DUSK OF DRAGONS

A COURT FOR THIEVES (Book #2)
A SONG FOR ORPHANS (Book #3)
A DIRGE FOR PRINCES (Book #4)
A JEWEL FOR ROYALS (BOOK #5)
A KISS FOR QUEENS (BOOK #6)
A CROWN FOR ASSASSINS (Book #7)
A CLASP FOR HEIRS (Book #8)

OF CROWNS AND GLORY
SLAVE, WARRIOR, QUEEN (Book #1)
ROGUE, PRISONER, PRINCESS (Book #2)
KNIGHT, HEIR, PRINCE (Book #3)
REBEL, PAWN, KING (Book #4)
SOLDIER, BROTHER, SORCERER (Book #5)
HERO, TRAITOR, DAUGHTER (Book #6)
RULER, RIVAL, EXILE (Book #7)
VICTOR, VANQUISHED, SON (Book #8)

KINGS AND SORCERERS
RISE OF THE DRAGONS (Book #1)
RISE OF THE VALIANT (Book #2)
THE WEIGHT OF HONOR (Book #3)
A FORGE OF VALOR (Book #4)
A REALM OF SHADOWS (Book #5)
NIGHT OF THE BOLD (Book #6)

THE SORCERER'S RING
A QUEST OF HEROES (Book #1)
A MARCH OF KINGS (Book #2)
A FATE OF DRAGONS (Book #3)
A CRY OF HONOR (Book #4)
A VOW OF GLORY (Book #5)
A CHARGE OF VALOR (Book #6)
A RITE OF SWORDS (Book #7)
A GRANT OF ARMS (Book #8)

DUSK OF DRAGONS

(Age of the Sorcerers-Book Six)

MORGAN RICE

MORGAN RICE

M organ Rice is the #1 bestselling and USA Today bestselling author of the epic fantasy series THE SORCERER'S RING, comprising seventeen books; of the #1 bestselling series THE VAMPIRE JOURNALS, comprising twelve books; of the #1 bestselling series THE SURVIVAL TRILOGY, a post-apocalyptic thriller comprising three books; of the epic fantasy series KINGS AND SORCERERS, comprising six books; of the epic fantasy series OF CROWNS AND GLORY, comprising eight books; of the epic fantasy series A THRONE FOR SISTERS, comprising eight books; of the new science fiction series THE INVASION CHRONICLES, comprising four books; of the fantasy series OLIVER BLUE AND THE SCHOOL FOR SEERS, comprising four books; of the fantasy series THE WAY OF STEEL, comprising four books; and of the new fantasy series AGE OF THE SORCERERS, comprising six books (and counting). Morgan's books are available in audio and print editions, and translations are available in over 25 languages.

TURNED (Book #1 in the Vampire Journals), ARENA 1 (Book #1 of the Survival Trilogy), A QUEST OF HEROES (Book #1 in the Sorcerer's Ring), RISE OF THE DRAGONS (Kings and Sorcerers—Book #1), A THRONE FOR SISTERS (Book #1), TRANSMISSION (The Invasion Chronicles—Book #1), and THE MAGIC FACTORY (Oliver Blue and the School for Seers—Book One) are each available as a free download on Amazon!

Morgan loves to hear from you, so please feel free to visit www.morganricebooks.com to join the email list, receive a free book, receive free giveaways, download the free app, get the latest exclusive news, connect on Facebook and Twitter, and stay in touch!

SELECT ACCLAIM FOR MORGAN RICE

"If you thought that there was no reason left for living after the end of THE SORCERER'S RING series, you were wrong. In RISE OF THE DRAGONS Morgan Rice has come up with what promises to be another brilliant series, immersing us in a fantasy of trolls and dragons, of valor, honor, courage, magic and faith in your destiny. Morgan has managed again to produce a strong set of characters that make us cheer for them on every page.... Recommended for the permanent library of all readers that love a well-written fantasy."

—*Books and Movie Reviews*
Roberto Mattos

"An action packed fantasy sure to please fans of Morgan Rice's previous novels, along with fans of works such as THE INHERITANCE CYCLE by Christopher Paolini.... Fans of Young Adult Fiction will devour this latest work by Rice and beg for more."

—*The Wanderer, A Literary Journal* (regarding *Rise of the Dragons*)

"A spirited fantasy that weaves elements of mystery and intrigue into its story line. *A Quest of Heroes* is all about the making of courage and about realizing a life purpose that leads to growth, maturity, and excellence....For those seeking meaty fantasy adventures, the protagonists, devices, and action provide a vigorous set of encounters that focus well on Thor's evolution from a dreamy child to a young adult facing impossible odds for survival....Only the beginning of what promises to be an epic young adult series."

—*Midwest Book Review* (D. Donovan, eBook Reviewer)

"THE SORCERER'S RING has all the ingredients for an instant success: plots, counterplots, mystery, valiant knights, and blossoming relationships replete with broken hearts, deception and betrayal. It will keep you entertained for hours, and will satisfy all ages. Recommended for the permanent library of all fantasy readers."

—*Books and Movie Reviews*, Roberto Mattos

"In this action-packed first book in the epic fantasy Sorcerer's Ring series (which is currently 14 books strong), Rice introduces readers to 14-year-old Thorgrin "Thor" McLeod, whose dream is to join the Silver Legion, the elite knights who serve the king…. Rice's writing is solid and the premise intriguing."

—*Publishers Weekly*

TABLE OF CONTENTS

CHAPTER ONE

Master Grey staggered down the street, close to death. The king's sorcerer had to grab for a wall to steady himself and keep from collapsing. He stumbled on, making his way from one solid point to the next, knowing that if he fell, he wouldn't get up.

He limped his way through the doorway of an abandoned building as daylight returned to Royalsport. Sweat beaded on his bald head with the effort, and he leaned on a length of wood he found, using it for support as he made his way inside.

The building seemed to be empty, which was probably just as well. Grey didn't have the energy left to convince anyone to leave him be, and he was sure that Emperor Ravin would pay handsomely for the former king's sorcerer. He smiled bitterly; unless he rested soon, Ravin's people wouldn't have to do anything to kill him.

He slumped against the wall for a second or two, then forced himself to climb through the house. Everything hurt in the wake of his fight with the Hidden, and there were sections of stairs where he had to all but crawl.

Grey passed by room after room until he came to a bedroom set at the very top of the house, possessions scattered on a broad bed as if someone had taken what they could in a hurry. There was a jug of cheap wine set on a table by the bed, and Master Grey sipped it, then spat it out, tasting brackish water mixed with his own blood. It had obviously been sitting there since the invasion.

The room had broad, arched windows that let in the sunlight. They also gave him a good spot from which to slump against the wall and look out over the city as the sun rose. He stared out at Royalsport's houses and its open spaces, taking in all the spaces that lay between its walls and beyond. Master Grey knew Royalsport as well as any man alive—all that it had been, all that it was, perhaps even what it would be.

He ached as he looked out through its windows, and that ache felt bone deep, pain coming from every atom of his being in the wake of his fight with the Hidden, and the dragon attack that had scoured the city with fire.

Master Grey could still see the aftermath of that attack as he stared out, seeing the points where fires still smoldered in the noble district and the market space around the House of Merchants, the slums and the space around the House of Weapons. In too many spots, there were still full flames, consuming buildings as people could only watch, looking on while all they owned burned.

In other parts, people were moving from island to island within the city, wading across the streams since they were at low tide. Many were carrying buckets, and Grey saw a whole chain of them heading in the direction of the House of Sighs' colorful exterior, putting out what remained of the dragon fire in Royalsport's interior.

To all the people there, it must have seemed like one more disaster piled upon the terror of the invasion. They'd seen their city fall, their former queen killed for attempting an uprising. The news had gone around that the princesses Lenore and Erin had been killed by Quiet Men. They'd had to endure the repression brought by the regime, with food and young men taken for the army, coin seized in taxes or simple plunder. Even now, the castle stood closed off, its gates shut, no help coming from it for those whose homes burned or whose families lay dead in the wake of the assault.

Grey could only imagine their terror as the dragon had attacked, although he'd felt his own share of it as it had hovered overhead. He'd been grateful for it too, though. In the moment when it had struck, his conflict against the Hidden had been...

He'd been going to die. There, he could admit that much to himself, at least. For all the power and knowledge he'd built in the course of a long life, he'd been just moments away from death. All three of the Hidden together had been too much for him to take on alone. Without the intervention of the dragon, he would have lost, would have been killed.

Grey sat there at the top of the building he'd found, contemplating his mortality in a way that he hadn't in a long time. He'd very rarely had any reason to, when magic had kept him safe, extended his life, let him do incredible things. He'd seen some of the dangers of what was coming, but now he could feel the weight of them pressing down on him, exhausting and draining as all the rest of it. Grey slumped against the frame of the window, using it to hold himself up.

His white robes were filthy now, edged with soot and marred by mud in the spots where he'd fallen. Ordinarily, he would have used magic to wipe those traces away, or at least disguise them, but now he didn't even have the strength for that.

Everything had fallen apart: Renard and the amulet were gone, the city was aflame, he was exhausted. The dragon over the city was a sign that things were unfolding as he had feared for so long, and now, he wasn't sure if he could see a way for things to turn out as they should.

No, he wouldn't give in to despair. There were still things to inspire hope in the middle of all of this.

For one thing, Wrath of the Hidden was dead, reduced to no more than ashes by the breath of the dragon. A world with one fewer of the Hidden in it was a better place; the dark powers that they trafficked with made them far too dangerous to be out there freely.

There were two left now: Void and Verdant. Both were still deadly, of course, and Void was probably the most dangerous of all of them. Taking them on would still be a huge task. Even so, Grey knew that he would need to do it at some point. He couldn't allow two sorcerers with such dangerous powers to continue to hunt for the amulet. If Verdant got it, the creeping madness he'd seen behind her eyes would be deadly enough, but if Void did ... no, he couldn't even contemplate that.

The other piece of good news was that Renard had clearly worked out how to use the amulet. The fact that the dragon wasn't still burning the city to the ground searching for it was proof of that, if nothing else. Someone had, at least, and who else but Renard would be able to hold the thing long enough to do so?

It meant that Renard was still out there, still alive, and still in possession of the amulet that had the potential to be their greatest weapon in the war to come. Others all had their parts to play in the things that would follow, but this was potentially more important than any of them.

Not for the first time, Grey wished that he had been able to keep the amulet somewhere other than in the depths of the hidden temple. Yet anywhere around people would have been too dangerous, too easy for the likes of the Hidden to get to, or for others to touch without knowing what it was. Even for him, the temptation had been great, only the knowledge of the way it could drain a man holding him back. The temple had been the safest place.

Now though, it wasn't anywhere safe. It was in Renard's hands, and Grey needed to find him.

He started with what seemed like the obvious approach for someone of his skills. Grey moved out into the room, taking a piece of chalk from a pocket, sketching symbols on the wooden floor of the room in which he stood, tracing the whorls of it by feel and memory.

He tried to touch the flow of the magic, tried to shape it to help him see. Forming a tracking spell meant tapping into the traces of the thing he wanted to find, and Grey's memory was filled with the feel of the amulet. He knew it as well as he knew the taste of the blood that still swirled in his mouth after his fight with the Hidden.

He spat that blood in the direction of his work, trying to throw a spark of power with it. In theory, the designs should shift as his magic struck it, blending and moving to point in the direction of the thief and the amulet he held. For a moment, Master Grey felt the simple piece of magic build...

Then it fizzled and failed, the magic fading. Master Grey cursed at that. How long had it been since one of his workings had failed to do *anything*? With all the time he'd had to learn his craft, ordinarily he found and held the delicate balance between the subtle elements of reality as well as any man who had lived. Now, he was so exhausted that he couldn't make a simple tracking charm work.

It didn't matter; he knew where he would be able to find Renard. He'd told the thief about the apparatus that lay in his tower, the one that would allow Grey to contain the power of the amulet so that it might be used safely in their cause. Since Renard had the amulet, he would be feeling its draining effects again, even though it was slower for him than for other men.

Grey had to hope that a man like Renard would be able to get into the castle, closed off as it was; that he would seek to use the apparatus, rather than casting the amulet aside for the likes of the Hidden to find.

His best hope was to get to his tower and meet Renard there, but to do that, he needed to get into the castle.

Ordinarily, it would have been little challenge for him; coming and going without being seen had been his wont for years.

Now, though, he could barely walk, and he did not have the strength for the most minor of magic.

Now, he was vulnerable.

CHAPTER TWO

Prince Greave woke on the edge of the forest, not far from Royalsport. He was sure that he would make it to the city today. He would get there, and he would find a way to avenge everything that had happened to his family. He would find a way to kill Emperor Ravin, even though the thought of killing still filled him with a sick feeling.

He'd done it now, though. He'd killed the woodsman who might have taken him there to the city as a prisoner. He'd given the man every chance, had *begged* him not to make him do it, but even so Greave had ended up killing him. He hadn't known that he'd had that hardness in him.

He got up and collected his few belongings, making sure that he had the vial of the cure that he'd produced, along with the secret to making more. He hadn't given up on finding Nerra. It was just that he needed to do this first.

He wondered if anyone would recognize him when he made it to the city. It didn't seem likely. He might have the same dark hair and almost feminine features as before, might be dressed in clothes that had once been noble, but he didn't look the same. His appearance was more ragged now, bearded and muddied by travel, his hair unkempt and his muscles hardened by the things he'd endured. He even felt like a different man than he had been.

He kicked the last embers of his campfire into darkness and set off through the last stretches of the woodland toward the city. When he reached the path, Greave moved quickly and quietly along it, his encounter with the woodsman he'd killed having taught him that he needed to be cautious.

It was because he was being cautious that he heard the sounds of men within the woods. He could hear their voices, and the sounds of their footfalls through the foliage. Greave froze in place for a moment, listening with all the caution of a wounded animal.

He darted into the trees, keeping out of sight. The sensible thing would probably be to slip away, but he couldn't do that if he didn't know where the people he was trying to avoid *were*. He picked his way across the forest floor, avoiding the dry twigs and brushwood that littered it.

He crept closer, and now the number of voices that he could hear multiplied, until it became a cacophony that was impossible to hide in the woodland. He could hear men shouting and giving commands, could hear the ring of steel as it was sharpened and even the sound of a voice or two raised in song.

Now it wasn't just a question of avoiding those who were there; now, he need to know what was going on. All knowledge had a use, and Greave wasn't about to let this piece fall by the wayside. He suspected that even Aurelle wouldn't have told him to walk the other way. Her curiosity as a spy would have made her need to know what was happening.

In any case, from where he was, the sounds lay between Greave and the city. He would have to get closer if only so that he could see how wide he needed to go in order to get around. Crouching low, Greave scurried through the woodland.

It was hard to imagined that he'd gotten to the point where he could do this, hard to imagine that he'd done almost any of the things that he had on his journey. He'd fought dangerous creatures and escaped burning cities. He'd piloted a raft to a deserted island and found a cure for a disease everyone saw as a death sentence. He'd lived in the wild, and he'd killed. Now, he was creeping toward the sound of armed men the way a scout might, approaching through the shadows of the trees until he was close enough to see...

...to see the army that was there.

There was no other word for it. An army was there in the forest, looking like it had come from some deeper point beyond Royalsport. Greave could see men and women there, some who looked like poorly armed peasants, others well-equipped men at arms. There were tents there, and horses, men training and others making repairs to their weapons or armor.

Greave's mind couldn't make sense of what he was seeing. There was no clear set of colors to mark the army, although he thought that he recognized the emblems of a few of the nobles. What did that mean? Had nobles risen up against the invasion from the Southern Kingdom, or were they acting on King Ravin's behalf, hunting out those who might fight against him? There was no way to know for sure without exposing himself to danger.

Greave stood there for several seconds, emotions roiling within him as he tried to decide what to do next. He guessed that Rodry would have stepped forward and proclaimed himself, taking the risk, but Rodry was dead. Likely all his family were dead. Grief flashed through Greave at that thought, and he knew that he wasn't going to risk this. Curiosity was one thing, but for now, it was better to get to the city. There, he would have a better idea of just who his friends were.

Greave started to move around the encampment, skirting the edges and moving cautiously through the trees. He was still doing it when a voice called out to him.

"Hold!"

Greave tensed to run, and the moment he did so an arrow thudded into a tree trunk next to him.

"Hold, I said!"

Two men came out of the trees, holding short hunting bows. A part of Greave said to run anyway, fear insisting that he was dead if he stayed there. The more sensible part of him knew that he had no way to outrun an arrow. He stood there, hands spread, carefully avoiding any weapons.

"Who are you?" one of the men demanded. "What are you doing, sneaking around our camp?"

If Greave had been sure about who the men were and what side they were on, he would have known what to do next. If he could have been certain that they were friends, he could have announced himself. If he knew they were Ravin's men, he would have at least known what lie to tell. As it was, he couldn't say anything, so he didn't.

"Talk!" the other man said.

"Why don't you tell me who *you* are?" Greave countered. "Whose camp is this?"

The first of the two scouts laughed at that. "Like you don't know. You weren't going for a gentle stroll through the forest, friend. You were skulking, trying to see our numbers."

"We should put an arrow in him, Colm," the other scout said. "Claim we found him and shot him when he tried to run. It's simpler all round."

"Simpler, but not smarter, Will," the first one said. "We don't know how many more like him there are out here, or who else knows about us."

While they were talking, Greave saw his chance. He ran for a break in the trees, keeping his head low, cutting left and right. He heard an arrow thud into a trunk beside him, felt his heart hammer in his chest at just how close it was to him. He didn't slow. He dodged around another tree trunk, felt another arrow whisper past his ear, too close for comfort.

Greave took another turning, realizing his mistake as a tree root caught his foot. He went tumbling, and as fast as he tried to rise, the two scouts were faster. They were on him before he could regain his footing, a boot clipping the side of his skull, a fist striking him in the ribs. Greave saw stars as they pressed him down, forcing his hands behind his back and tying him with a spare bow string that cut into his flesh with its tightness.

"I *told* you we should have just shot him," Will said.

"Shut up," the other, Colm, replied. "If he's run, it's because he knows something. We need to take him to the camp and find out what that is."

"We could just get it out of him here," Will said. "Quiet Men might be tough, but I reckon that when you've hit him enough, this one will talk."

"Quiet Men?" Greave managed between gasps for air. "I'm not—"

The scout hit him then, cutting off his words.

"Enough," Will said. "We'll take him to the queen. She'll want to know about this. She'll probably reward us for catching this one."

The queen? What queen? Greave's mind raced, trying to make sense of the words, but his head was still ringing with the impact of being hit, and in any case, he wasn't sure what to think. Had Ravin taken a bride to secure his hold over the Northern Kingdom? Was that what this was? Had he stumbled on the protection for a Wedding Harvest?

The scouts dragged him to his feet and then all but carried him back in the direction of the encampment. They took him to a tent that sat in the middle of it all, where a couple of guards stood there, leaning on spears.

"We found a Quiet Man," Colm said. "Figured the queen would want to see him before she has him executed."

Executed? Fear filled Greave then, at the thought that he might die before he could finish all that he was there to do. He'd come there to bring down Ravin, but what if he found himself cut down before he even reached Royalsport?

At a nod from the guards, the two scouts who held Greave dragged him into the tent, where a dark-haired figure stood, resplendent and clearly in command. They threw Greave down at her feet, and as he looked up at her, he had a moment of shocked disbelief, his mind refusing to accept that he was staring up into the features of someone he'd been certain was dead, someone whose face he knew as well as his own.

"Lenore?"

CHAPTER THREE

L enore stared down at her brother in shock, unable to believe for a moment that it was really him. Judging by the way he said her name, he couldn't believe it either.

One of the scouts who had brought him in lifted a fist as if he was going to strike Greave. "Don't you talk to the queen like that, you Quiet Man filth!"

Lenore stepped forward, stopping the blow. "That's no Quiet Man; that's my *brother*!"

The scout stepped back, hurrying to apologize, but Lenore was too busy helping her brother to his feet.

"Go," she said.

"Yes, my queen," the men said in unison, and left the tent.

Lenore stared at her brother for a second or two, then wrapped him in her arms, unable to find the words for how happy she was. For a moment, it seemed as if they were both speaking over one another, trying to express their joy, their surprise, their shock.

Greave pulled back to arm's length, staring at her as if he couldn't believe that she was there. Lenore knew the feeling.

"It's really you," Greave said. "You're alive."

"I feel like I should be saying that to *you*," Lenore said. Her brother had been missing for so long that a part of her had started to assume the worst. She could feel tears in her eyes that she was sure a queen shouldn't shed, but right then she was too overwhelmed at the thought of her brother still being alive to stop them.

She could see tears to match them in Greave's eyes.

"They said you were dead," he said, voice filled with emotion. "I heard... I heard that the new emperor had ordered you murdered by his Quiet Men."

"He did," Lenore said. "But I survived. Erin too. We managed to get away, but he spread the lie that we were dead so that we couldn't rebel."

"Does that mean that Erin is here too?" Greave asked, and the happiness in his voice made Lenore smile. Greave had always been so serious, so darkly thoughtful about everything.

"She's not here," Lenore said. "We think... we think she went off to try to kill Ravin." She thought for a moment and realized that she should get her brother out of the bonds that held him. She moved behind him and cut him free with a knife. He winced and rubbed his wrists.

"And your mother?" Greave asked. "Are the rumors about Queen Aethe's execution..."

Lenore choked back a sound of pain at the thought of what had happened to her mother. Greave put his arms around her, holding her close for a moment or two.

"I'm sorry," he said as he pulled back. "She... I didn't always get on with her, but she deserved better than that."

"She did," Lenore said, and this time the tears she wiped from her eyes came from grief and pain.

"What about you?" she asked. "Where have you *been,* Greave? You look so... so different."

He barely looked like her brother anymore. The Greave who had left to try to find a way to help their sister had been a gentle, bookish young man. This version of him seemed harder and rougher around the edges.

"I went looking for a cure for Nerra," he said. "I went to Astare with... with Aurelle."

Lenore remembered the young woman who had become so close to Greave in the days before he'd left. The pain in Greave's voice as he said her name was palpable.

"What happened?" Lenore asked.

"She turned out to be a spy, sent to kill me," Greave said. "But... she saved my life too. Without her I wouldn't have made it to the library of Astare, wouldn't have gotten out. She's... she's gone."

It sounded to Lenore like they both had so much to catch up on. At the same time, she could hear the soldiers outside as they packed up the camp. She saw the tent flap open, and a messenger stepped in.

"Forgive me, my queen," the man said. "But General Odd would like to speak with you."

"Greave," she said, taking his hand. "There's a lot I have to tell you, a lot that's happening, but there's one part you need to know for now: I have been gathering allies, and I mean to take back this kingdom."

"I heard them call you queen," Greave said.

Lenore had a moment of fear at that. Technically, Greave was older than her, and a son to the old king rather than a daughter. There were those who might see that as a reason for Greave to rule, and not her.

Greave must have seen Lenore's worry, because he closed his hands over hers. "You will be a much better ruler than I could ever hope to be," he said. "I've seen the people out there. They've found someone to inspire them, to give them hope. They need that, not someone like me."

Lenore sighed with relief. "Thank you, but I'm pretty sure we'll need your help too. Will you walk with me to talk with Odd? He used to be a knight. He has protected me and Erin, and now he's my general."

"Of course," Greave said. "You're planning to attack Royalsport?"

"That's the idea," Lenore said. "Come on, walk with me."

She led the way outside, to where her forces were gathered. There were so many people there: villagers who had volunteered when they'd heard the rumors of her being alive, former bandits and soldiers who had volunteered because they had nowhere else to go. Men from the retinues of the nobles who had come to her banner stood with the rest, well armed and well trained. They started to flock around her as she walked through the camp, messengers coming from all sides with notices about their food supplies or the latest people to join their forces, the layout of the camp or the rate of travel. Lenore did her best to walk between it all and keep moving. Greave walked beside her, and his presence seemed to mean that they kept back, giving her the room to walk.

Lenore could see Greave looking around at them, and there was a thoughtful expression on her brother's face. Lenore could also see the hint of worry there.

They made it across the camp, to a spot where a man stood wearing what appeared to be the robes of a monk over a chain shirt, although those robes seemed to have been roughly made from whatever was on hand. They were brown with mud and gray with wear. His hair was shaven and he had no beard, and he was larger than most men would have been. A longsword rested incongruously against a camp table, on which a map of Royalsport was set. The monk was staring down at it, and he had a worried expression. He looked up, and then bowed as Lenore and Greave approached.

"Your majesty," he said.

"Odd, you don't have to do that," Lenore told him, as it felt like she'd told him a hundred times in the last day or two. She swept a hand in Greave's direction. "Odd, I want to introduce you to Greave."

She saw the former monk's eyes widen. "*Prince* Greave? He's alive? My queen, what does that mean?"

"It means nothing except that I'm here to help," Greave said, taking a step forward.

Lenore saw Odd visibly relax as her brother said that. "Not that I'm much use with a sword."

"We need more than that," Odd said. He didn't look happy.

Lenore frowned. "What's wrong, Odd?"

Greave guessed it before she did. "You don't have enough men."

It caught Lenore a little by surprise to hear him say it, but she saw Odd nod his head, however reluctantly.

"For a frontal assault, yes," he said. "I am sorry, Lenore. I have failed you."

Lenore could hear the shame there, and she knew how important it was to Odd to do his part in this. Yet she felt shame of her own as he said that.

"It's not your fault," she said. "If I'd brought in more people ..."

"You have brought in more soldiers in a shorter space of time than I could have believed possible," Odd said. "You've brought together commoners and nobles, soldiers and ordinary folk. Your mother managed a conspiracy of noblemen, and your brother Rodry might have been able to lead knights, but *you* have drawn together *everyone*."

It still wasn't enough, though. Lenore sighed. "Could we wait for more people?"

Even as she asked the question, she knew the answer. If they waited, they would have to find food for an army, while there was more chance of Ravin finding out about her efforts and sending out a force to kill them all. Worse, the longer this went on, the more people would drift away from their cause. This only worked while she had their enthusiasm.

"The problem is Royalsport's defenses?" Greave asked, beside Lenore. "The rivers and the bridges as well as the walls?"

Lenore saw her new general nod. He looked a little surprised, as if he hadn't expected Greave to guess the problem. But then, her brother wasn't exactly renowned as a warrior.

"The city was designed to be defensible," Odd said. "Even in the initial invasion, when we'd lost most of the knights, we still made them pay for each step."

"Could we get in through the river channels when the streams are at low tide?" Greave asked.

Lenore's eyebrows rose at that. "That's how Ravin's forces invaded."

Her brother hadn't known that, and he'd guessed the same strategy as one of the greatest military minds of the age.

"Which means that he'll be ready for anyone trying the same thing," Greave said. "Sorry, I should leave this to the people who know more."

That gave Lenore an idea, though.

"No, I think you are exactly the person for this task," Lenore said.

She saw her brother start to shake his head, saw Odd frown at the idea of the bookish Prince Greave trying to help. She spoke up before either of them could say anything.

"Greave, Odd," she said. "If we can't take them on head on, we need to find a strategy that will work. Who better than the two of you, working together. Odd, you're one of the greatest knights to ever live."

"I'm renowned for my fury more than my strategy," Odd pointed out.

"And I'm not known even for *that*," Greave said.

"No, you're known for being the cleverest of all of us," Lenore replied. "Are you going to tell me that you haven't read every book about strategy?"

"Maybe a few," Greave said. "Even so, I—"

"You're clever," Lenore said, not giving him a chance to make the excuse. "And we *need* clever right now. Odd can tell you what will work militarily, but we need ideas, and there's no one better at those than you."

Her brother and Odd both nodded their assent. Lenore felt a surge of hope at that. She knew that she could inspire her troops, and that Odd could be there when the fighting grew most dangerous. Now, with all her brother's cleverness to help them plan, they had a chance.

CHAPTER FOUR

A urelle came back to consciousness and for a moment the world was nothing but darkness and pressure. It seemed to crush in all around her, and for several seconds she couldn't remember why.

Briefly, beautifully, she imagined herself under the covers of Greave's bed back at the castle. He would come to find her soon, and draw the covers back off her head. He would kiss her back to wakefulness, and ...

The dream was so sweet that Aurelle didn't want it to end, but memory intruded all too soon. She remembered the dragon attack, and the child she'd been trying to get to safety. She remembered the collapsing building, the tumble of joists and bricks around her.

"Help!" Aurelle cried out, and for the first time in what seemed like the longest time, she panicked. She thrashed around in the dark, trying to get free of the things pinning her in place, but none of it would move, the weight was too great. "Help!"

She didn't panic, not like this, but the thought of being trapped beneath a collapsed building was simply too much. She couldn't stand the thought of being trapped, of being held in place, of not being able to *do* anything. All the time she'd spent in the House of Sighs, there had been the sense that she was doing something valuable in the world, affecting things even if it sometimes meant doing things that she would never have chosen.

Now, she couldn't do anything, couldn't affect anything. She pushed and shoved at the things around her, but nothing gave, even a little. She tried to call for help, but none came. Aurelle could feel her breathing running faster and faster, her heart thudding in her chest.

17

No, she would not die here, like this. She would *not*, when her revenge against the men who had done so much damage to this kingdom was still incomplete. Aurelle knew that she needed to control herself, and stop thrashing in case she brought down the whole weight of the house on whatever little pocket of space she was caught in.

She imagined Greave there with her, imagined the comfort of his touch, the softness of his voice. The thought of him there stilled her, calmed her, even as it reminded her why she needed to stay alive. What would Greave do in a situation like this? He would stay calm, and he would think.

So Aurelle thought. She knew that she was under the weight of too much rubble to move it, or her thrashing efforts would already have brought her to freedom. She knew that she had air, because she wasn't dead yet, but how much? She couldn't feel any breeze on her skin, so what if the air trapped in this space with her was all she had left?

Aurelle forced herself to slow her breathing, staying still, using as little energy as she could. All she could do was try to last as long as she could, stay still, and hope for rescue.

What rescue? Who in the world would care enough to try to get her out of here? She wanted to believe that Meredith would send people for her if she knew, but she had no way of knowing that a house had fallen on her. Other than that, who?

Greave would have come for her; Aurelle wanted to believe that even though he'd sent her away, and told her that he couldn't trust her. If he hadn't died back on the docks of Astare, she wanted to believe that he would have come to save her, not letting anything stop him. He wouldn't have torn the rubble from above her with his hands, because that wasn't Greave, but he *would* have come up with some kind of clever mechanism or found the perfect spot to apply force to free her.

Aurelle lay there then, and cried in the darkness for all that she'd lost. She lay there, still and silent, unable to do anything for what seemed like an eternity.

Then, above her, she heard people.

"Help!" she called. "Help!"

"Hold on," a voice called back. "We'll get you out of there."

Hands pulled at the rubble around her, moving aside bricks, lifting aside the large lengths of wood that pinned Aurelle in place. Light flooded in, and after the darkness before it was enough to hurt Aurelle's eyes.

A figure stood above her, and for one beautiful moment, she thought that Greave was standing there. The man there was slender and dark-haired in the same way, tall and reaching down for her. Yet as Aurelle saw more clearly, she realized that it was just one of a group of men who had come to help.

She managed to stand, brushing dust from her dress and from the red of her hair. There were scratches across most of her skin now, and she blinked as she looked round at the people. She paused as she recognized the little girl standing there. She was the one Aurelle had saved out in the streets.

"Meredith sent us," the man said. "When the girl arrived, we couldn't really understand what she was saying, but she insisted that you were out here."

"Thank you," Aurelle said. She went over to the girl. "And thank *you*. You saved my life."

The girl smiled shyly and took Aurelle's hand as they headed back in the direction of the House of Sighs. It stood, colorful and bright, above the ruins around it. People from it were in the streets, trying to help where they could, putting out fires and handing out food to the ones who needed it.

"Let's take you back," Aurelle said to the girl, who nodded. Aurelle looked around at the men who had come to help her. "Will you come with us?"

"Lady Meredith has other tasks for us to perform," the man said. "There is a lot to do today. The castle is closed off, with no help from it."

Aurelle could only imagine what that was like, with everyone fighting to deal with the aftermath of the dragon attack, and no help coming from the emperor or his cronies. At a time like this, if the rulers of the kingdom weren't helping, then it was left to the people of Royalsport to help one another. The House of Sighs was a good place to coordinate that and make sure that everyone got the help that they needed.

For now, she needed to get back to the House and see what was happening. Before, it had been a simple case of reporting back, but now, with everything that had happened, Aurelle wasn't sure *what* was going on.

Still holding the girl's hand, she headed back in the direction of the House of Sighs. It was only a short way, and even in that distance she could see plenty of people trying to deal with the aftermath of the attack. There were people rooting through the rubble, checking for other survivors, although Aurelle saw few of those. She saw far *more* spots where bodies were being pulled from the wreckage, some crushed, some burned beyond recognition. She tried to turn the girl's head away from the worst of it, but she knew that she would see some of it.

Aurelle tried to imagine what life would be like for this girl as they reached the House of Sighs. Right now, this was the only safe place for her, but what kind of life would there be for her? Would she end up like Aurelle? Would there be a world for her to be anything else? If she and the others didn't change things, then what kind of world would there be for this girl to grow up in?

Aurelle hammered on one of the side doors, and a tired-looking young man opened it. He was clearly one of the House's servants, and had the look of someone who more normally would have been receiving patrons, yet now he looked as if he'd been up all night, trying to help with everything that had been happening in the city. He nodded an acknowledgment as Aurelle came in.

"Take this girl and make sure that she's safe and fed," Aurelle said. She turned to the girl. "Thank you for saving me. We'll do our best to keep you safe here, and if you ever need anything, you only *ever* have to ask. Do you understand?"

The girl nodded.

"I'm Aurelle," Aurelle said. She took the girl's hand.

"Maisie," the girl said.

"Go on, Maisie," Aurelle said. "I'll find you later."

The servant led the girl away, and Aurelle wished that she could go with her. She'd just had a building fall on her. She was hurt and she was tired. She wanted nothing more than to go and find somewhere to sleep, find something to eat, yet she knew that she would need to talk to Meredith first. She needed to find out what was happening, and what they were all going to do next. She had the feeling that the events in the city were moving forward faster now, and that meant that there was no time in which to pause.

She headed up through the House, where rooms that would ordinarily have been given over to pleasure now seemed to have been commandeered for medicine and shelter, feeding people and simply providing somewhere safe. She reached Meredith's rooms, and seemed to have arrived just in time to walk in on an argument.

"...told you that you were supposed to stay here and do nothing!" Meredith shouted. Dark-haired and in her thirties, she looked poised and composed in spite of everything that had been happening.

Aurelle walked in and saw Renard there, broad and red-haired, muscled and surprisingly sheepish looking in the face of Meredith's anger. Orianne was there too, Princess Lenore's former maidservant looking poised and ready to play her part in everything that was to come.

She *wasn't* expecting the third figure, who sat trying to fit the head of a spear to a new short staff. She was slender and athletic, with short dark hair and features that Aurelle had seen many times around the castle when she'd been there with Greave.

"Princess Erin?" she said.

Erin looked up at her. "Aurelle? You're the one who was with my brother, aren't you? Where is he? Where's Greave?"

It felt like a stone lodged in Aurelle's heart as she answered. "I'm sorry," she said. "He... he's dead."

CHAPTER FIVE

E rin flinched as the red-haired noblewoman told her that her brother was dead. She'd feared for him in the time that he'd been missing, but to actually hear it... it was one more drop of hurt, poured into an ocean of it.

"No," she whispered. She felt so tired, so broken in that moment, and not just physically. All the spots where Ravin had battered at her, the ribs that felt as if they might be broken, the wounds at her sides and along her arms, felt like nothing compared to that.

"He died on the docks at Astare," Aurelle said, and she sounded almost as hurt as Erin was.

One question came to Erin then. "Wait, what are you doing here?"

"Aurelle is one of my people," Meredith said. "She always was."

Erin stared at Meredith then, and at Aurelle. She felt her hand tighten on her spear.

"So you tricked him into thinking that you loved him?" she said. "You were deceiving him all along?"

She started to move forward, and in spite of her exhaustion she was still quick enough to put the blade of her spear to the woman's throat. To her surprise, though, there was a knife in Aurelle's hand, the tip of it pressed to Erin's stomach.

Meredith was there too. "Aurelle, tell Princess Erin what you felt about her brother, please."

Erin saw the pain in Aurelle's eyes as she responded.

"I loved him," Aurelle said. "I loved him more than anything, and I spent most of the time I was with him hating myself for the betrayal. I saved his life, and he saved mine, and then... I saw him die, and it broke my heart. You can't know what that's like."

Except that Erin *did* know what that was like. It was feeling helpless, hating yourself for not being able to do anything about it. Hating the world for not being different. It was wanting to kill the people responsible for it. She wanted to say all of that, but didn't.

"You'd be surprised," she said, instead.

She pulled her spear blade away from Aurelle's throat. In that moment, she felt more kinship than she could have believed for this woman.

"Erin," Meredith said. "You look exhausted. Would you like somewhere to sleep, something to eat?"

Erin shook her head. She couldn't sleep now, and she didn't have any appetite, not with everything that had happened. She wanted… she didn't know *what* she wanted.

No, she *did* know, and it turned out that it was impossible. She wanted Ravin dead, and she'd failed. She'd done her best to finish him, and in the end the only reason she'd survived had been because the dragon had attacked. Even then, she'd only escaped with Renard's help. Now, she had to live with the shame of that failure.

She winced as she went to sit back down.

"At least let us dress your wounds," Orianne said. Her sister's former maid moved briskly, bandaging the spots where Ravin had cut her, wrapping her ribs tightly to hold them stable, stitching one wound on her flank that was too deep for just a bandage. Erin winced as the needle slid in and out of her flesh, determined that she wouldn't cry out with the pain.

"I need to get out of the city," she said.

Meredith looked over at her, and Erin caught the note of suspicion there in her expression. "Why? Why not remain here with us? We can keep you hidden well enough within the House."

Erin shook her head. She needed to get back to her sister. The trouble was that she didn't dare *say* that, not here, not now. She might have had a moment of understanding with Aurelle that had kept Erin from killing her, and Renard might have saved her life, but this was still a place of lies and betrayal, where information was valued mostly for what others would give to hear it. She couldn't just give away Lenore's location, or the fact that she was building an army.

She heard Meredith sigh. "Let me guess; there are things you can't say."

Erin nodded.

"That is the hardest part, sometimes," Meredith said. "Knowing who to trust. Take Renard here. Everything I know about him says that he is utterly chaotic and untrustworthy, that his very presence is likely to result in disaster. I gave him the simplest of instructions, to remain in my House and draw no attention to himself, yet instead he went out into the city."

"Meredith," Renard began, "that's not exactly—"

"But if he had not done so, you would not be here," Meredith said. "That you stand in opposition to Ravin is obvious enough, so let me set out what *we* are doing."

Erin saw her point to Orianne.

"Orianne here has been trying to find any lingering friends within the city who might prove loyal in the event of an uprising. As you can imagine it has been hard finding anyone, but Orianne is finding those who remain."

Erin felt a brief hint of hope at that, but she knew how few allies there would be left in the city. Ravin's murderous response to her mother's rebellion had seen to that.

"Then there's Aurelle," Meredith said. "She has been sowing dissent among those who have allied themselves to Ravin, trying to find ways to pull nobles away from him. Have you succeeded, Aurelle?"

Erin saw Aurelle shrug.

"I believe that Duke Viris and his son are now considering the position that their support of the new emperor has left them in," she said.

"And I have done my own work to try to sow dissent," Meredith said. She looked over to Erin. "We have been making preparations, princess, but we do not know yet what we are making preparations *for*. We need direction; we need hope. I believe that you might be able to give us that."

"You're planning to make her a figurehead for a rebellion?" Renard asked. "Meredith, you can't—"

"She doesn't need to," Erin said. The decision was an easy one to make, now that she had heard all that she had heard. It was obvious that everyone here was as committed to overthrowing Ravin and his regime as she was. More than that, the things they were doing made it more likely that Lenore would succeed.

"What are you saying?" Meredith asked.

"I'm saying that my sister is alive and trying to gather an army," Erin said.

"She has an army?" Orianne said.

The truth was that Erin didn't know the answer to that. She *hoped* that Lenore would have an army by now, and there had definitely been people flowing in when she had left. Even so, she'd been hoping that it wouldn't be necessary, that she would simply kill Ravin and it would be done.

"She's been trying to gather one," Erin said. "I left before I saw what was happening. I thought... I thought I could end this cleanly."

A fresh wave of shame hit her. She'd failed. If she'd just been a little faster when she struck at Ravin, none of this would be needed.

"Now, though, I need to get back to her," Erin said.

She saw Meredith nod. "I think that's a good idea, but getting you out of the city would be difficult, especially in the wake of the dragon attack. In any case, you're wounded."

"Not badly," Erin said. She stood, testing how she felt. She was battered and bruised, but none of her injuries would be enough to stop her.

"I can help get her out," Renard said. He looked stronger than he had in the moments when he'd found Erin, somehow more alive.

"And you think I should trust you with something like this?" Meredith shot back.

"I thought you didn't want me in your precious House?" Renard retorted. Erin had no idea what the history was between the two of them, but it was obvious just looking at them that there *was* some. "In any case, it's... better if I don't stay in Royalsport right now."

"Why?" Meredith asked. "What did you do out in the city?"

Renard didn't answer that. To Erin, he looked like a guilty schoolboy.

"Look, it's just better if I go," he said. "Besides, who else can you spare? The last I heard your plans involved everyone else you trust working to disrupt Ravin's alliances."

"That implies that I trust you," Meredith said, but Erin could tell that it was bluster. Sure enough, a second or two later she gave a curt nod. "All right. You get the princess to her sister. Take whatever you need to be able to do it, and don't get caught. We won't be able to help if the Quiet Men get hold of you."

"As if anyone could ever catch me," Renard said.

Meredith sighed. "I'm going to regret this, aren't I?"

Erin didn't know about that, but she was glad that there would be *someone* helping her. On the way into the city, she'd felt invincible, certain that she could move through it unseen, determined to succeed in her mission. Now that she'd failed, everything felt uncertain, like the world was crumbling.

It took them a while to gather everything they needed. Erin took the time to finish the repairs to her snapped spear, and took a couple of short stabbing daggers to replace the ones she'd lost. Renard had a sword and a long knife hidden beneath a cloak, along with a pack with provisions for the journey.

It was perhaps a full hour before they were truly ready to leave the House of Sighs, and to Erin's surprise, Meredith herself came to see them off, meeting them by a small side door that offered the best chance of slipping into the city unseen. She turned to Erin first.

"When you reach your sister, tell her that Royalsport will be waiting for any move that she makes. I will try to get my people into position to help, and I will make sure that Ravin has fewer allies than he should."

Erin nodded, grateful for that, at least. Any help that they could have in a moment like this would matter.

"Just... don't take too long," Meredith said. "Ravin is cunning, and he is dangerous."

"I know how dangerous he is," Erin assured her.

"As for you," Meredith said, turning to Renard. Erin wasn't entirely surprised when she kissed him, although Renard looked more than surprised enough for both of them. "Get out of my House."

Erin led the way out of there, into the city. She'd failed in what she'd come to do, but maybe, just maybe, there was still a chance to get some good out of this.

Chapter Six

A round Devin, screams cut through the air, and the crackle of flames against wood. Timbers collapsed in buildings nearby, and people cried out as they struggled to get to safety. Everywhere he looked, there were fires, and people hurrying, trying to do *something* to help with the chaos.

He took a bucket from the pair of hands behind him in the chain he stood in, flinging the water within on the fire that burned in front of him. His dark hair was a mess now, his lean frame streaked with sweat and soot. He'd done it so many times that his arms ached from the effort now, and still the building in front of him burned.

Plenty did, here in the poorest parts of the city. The houses here were more wood than stone, and it wasn't as if Ravin's troops or the city guard were willing to help. The fires here weren't even close enough to any noble houses to be a threat to them, and in any case, the nobles had problems of their own.

Which left people helping one another. Devin took another bucket and threw water on the flames. He heard the hiss as it doused part of it, reducing the fire to something manageable, something that might not consume yet another home.

Not everywhere was so lucky. Devin heard a cry a little way away and turned, seeing a partly collapsed building that had been standing moments before. Abandoning the house he was working on, Devin ran in the direction of the house there, determined to save anyone he could.

He saw people there, a man and a woman trapped between the burning joists of the house, unable to get free. Without thinking, Devin tried to pull those joists away, then jerked back in pain. The heat of the flames was too much.

"There's nothing we can do," a man said beside Devin.

"No, there has to be *something*," Devin said. Around him, people were working on every side, helping one another, saving one another. Yet plenty had died during the night, burned or crushed when no one could save them. He *wouldn't* let these people die too.

Devin remembered the storm up on the mountaintop. He knelt, putting a hand against one of the few fragments of the burning house cool enough to touch. Before, he'd needed Sigil's touch to be able to fully touch the magic around him, but now panic pushed him into a space where he *saw* the fire, really saw it.

In seeing it, he understood. Devin knew the shifting balances of it, changing second by second, knew the hunger of it that pushed more harshly than even the bitter cold of the far north had.

Devin remembered what it had been like trying to tame that storm, the complexity of it and the effort. The fire was even more complex, because it was not one thing but a thousand, not one swirling mass governed by surprisingly simple laws, but point after point burning up independently. Trying to keep track of all that was … it *hurt*.

Devin felt the familiar sensation of fur under his fingers and heard the growl of a wolf as Sigil pressed against him. Ordinarily he would have expected people to reel back from the presence of a creature like that in the middle of Royalsport, but right then they were too busy dealing with the aftermath of the dragon's attack to even flinch at Sigil's presence.

"You knew I needed you," Devin breathed, wondering at the presence of the wolf, and what it implied about the connection between them. There was no time to say more, though, because the fire was still there, still burning, still threatening to consume the people within this house and so many more.

Devin reached for the fire and tried to work out what to balance within it, yet it didn't work like that. Fire didn't balance, it only built, only consumed. So what *did* balance with fire?

The answer came instantly, and Devin reached out for the sensation of the water running through Royalsport's rivers. He screamed as he became the conduit for that power, clinging to Sigil only with an effort of will as agony burst through him. For the briefest, purest moment, it felt as though he held all that energy.

Then Devin threw it into the fires around him.

He heard people gasp in shock as steam burst up from the fires, rising into the air, cooling, and then forming as a mist that seemed to envelop everything. The people around Devin became shadows in that mist, still passing buckets to one another, but now they were fighting the embers of the fires rather than a blazing mass of them.

Devin knelt in the middle of that for a moment, then reached into the house that had been burning, helping those within to safety. He leaned on them as much as they did on him in that moment, the sheer effort that it had taken to serve as a conduit for that much power hitting Devin all at once.

He helped them out of the house and then broke away from them, finding Sigil again and limping from the fire. He knew that people would start asking questions soon, even if they were currently busy trying to put out the last of the blazes. They would want to know where the sudden mist had come from and why fires around the city had been reduced to mere embers.

Was it the whole city? Certainly the fires around the poor district seemed to have been affected, but Devin had no way of knowing how his efforts had affected things up in the noble district, toward the castle. He couldn't see more than a dozen paces ahead of himself at the moment, and for all he knew, fires were still blazing everywhere he couldn't see.

He didn't think so, though. Devin had *felt* the moment when he'd balanced the forces in the city. He'd felt the power involved, and the spread of it. It might not be enough to stop the flames completely, but with the efforts of the people who were still working throughout the city, it had to be enough.

Devin found a patch of wall and rested against it, trying to get his strength back. Sigil was there by his side, but for the moment Devin didn't dare to touch the wolf in case the connection to his magic tempted him to try to do more. He'd used far too much power in the last few hours, both in trying to put out the fires and before that, in his battle with Anders.

29

Thoughts of the boy who had attacked him could creep back in now that the fires were under control. Anders had seemed to come out of nowhere, and Devin was still shocked by the things that he'd claimed: that he'd been a *second* boy picked out by Master Grey to play a part in all this, and that Devin had fulfilled a destiny he'd believed meant for him.

Devin didn't know the truth of that. He knew that Master Grey did not give straight answers, and that he was as likely to play games as to simply set things out honestly, but would he really send the two of them after the Unfinished Sword without telling either of them about the other's existence?

Thoughts of the sword made hurt and disappointment flare in Devin. He'd put so much work into the sword, had crafted it to perfection, only for Anders to steal it. There was a flash of anger at that thought, because it didn't feel right that Anders should just take the blade after all Devin's work, yet Devin wasn't sure what else to feel about the other boy. Anders hadn't seemed evil exactly, just aggrieved to the point where he wouldn't accept any solution other than violence.

Devin knew that he would need to find Anders at some point, and for a brief moment he tried to think of some way he might be able to do it with magic, the way it had been obvious that Anders had tracked him.

He knew, though, that he didn't need anything like that, not really. Devin knew what Anders wanted, and that meant that he knew where the other boy would be going. He'd heard the betrayal in the other boy's voice, heard him declare what he was going to do when he found Master Grey. Anders might or might not try to fulfill the destiny that had been set for him, but first he would try to kill Master Grey.

To do that, he would need to find him, and the most likely spot to begin was the sorcerer's tower. Anders would be heading there, and if Devin could get inside, he could find his would-be rival. Then... well, Devin hadn't thought that far ahead, but he would find a way to take back the sword. He needed it. The dragon attack had shown him the power of the sword, and the scale of the danger that might be coming. Without the sword, there might be no way to stop the threat.

Devin knew then where he needed to go. A part of him wanted to rush off to the tower right away, to get there before Anders did. He knew that getting inside would be difficult, but he had the advantage that he'd at least been in the castle and the tower before. He knew his way, and that had to count for something.

Even as he thought it, a young man ran up to him.

"Help! We need more pairs of hands to lift a joist. There's people trapped this way!"

Devin knew in that moment that he couldn't just abandon the people here. He had to help, couldn't just run off after his supposed destiny while there were still people trapped, still people hurt.

"I'm coming," he replied. He hurried off after the other young man. Anders would have to wait until Devin was sure the people of the city were safe. After that, though, Devin would find him—and the sword.

CHAPTER SEVEN

Anders smiled to himself as the mist fell over the city, feeling the magic of his would-be rival. It was like everything he'd seen from Devin: impressive in its way but undisciplined and untrained. How could Master Grey entrust a destiny to someone like that?

It didn't matter. Master Grey would be dead soon enough, and Anders would determine his *own* destiny. Perhaps he would even choose to be the hero that the old fool had seemed to want, but it would be *his* choice, not the sorcerer's.

He looked like a hero as he made his way through the streets of Royalsport. The silver charms bound into his short blond hair jangled, and his dark clothes were further stained with soot and dirt from the journey. He strode toward the castle, taller and broader than most of the people he passed.

"You, what are you doing there?" a guard on one of the bridges demanded. Anders just strode past him, and because he was moving quickly, he was lost in the mist again before the guard could move to stop him. Devin had done him a favor in that respect, even if he'd stolen so much else from Anders without even meaning to.

Anders could guess why the guard had challenged him; he was holding the sword openly in its scabbard, rather than hidden away under a cloak. In a recently conquered city that probably made him a threat. Anders briefly considered hiding the blade away beneath his cloak, but instead he just walked faster. He would be past any other guards before they realized what was happening, and in any case, he wanted to be ready in case any other danger struck at him.

Anders considered the sword. It had the word *Loss* embossed on it, and he guessed that was meant to be its name. Anders could feel the power running through it, along with a terrible sense of sadness as he held it. There was a darkness in this blade, but it suited some of the pain that still sat in Anders, all the things he felt at the loss of his friends and the leagues he'd walked for nothing mirrored in it.

Of course, it wasn't just the sword he had now. He took out the amulet he'd found, holding it carefully and keeping up what protections he could against the pull of it against his power. Perhaps he should have thrown it from himself the moment he found it, because it certainly felt dangerous enough, but Anders could also feel the power there, and he recognized the dragon scale at the heart of it for what it was.

Master Grey would know what the amulet was, and Anders would make sure that he told him, in the moments before the old man died.

First though, Anders needed to get to him. That was why he was heading for the castle. It was impossible to guess where the old king's sorcerer was at any given moment, but sooner or later he was going to return to that tower of his. When he did, he would find Anders waiting for him.

Anders kept going through the now mist-shrouded streets of the city. Around him, the shadows of people flickered here and there as they worked to rescue others or to put on the remaining fires. Anders was grateful that people were safe, but he didn't stop to help; he had his own business to see to, and that business was important enough that the fate of the whole kingdom might hinge upon it. In any case, this wasn't his city, and these weren't his people.

The walls of the castle loomed ahead now, and Anders found himself contemplating all the ways that there might be inside such a place. Hidden tunnels were always a possibility, since rulers so often seemed to want an escape route, but that would mean finding them. In any case, he had no doubt that an invader like Ravin would have them watched closely.

Scaling the walls was another option, but to do that, he would need to cross the river before the gates, and even in the mist it felt like there was too much of a chance of being spotted. No, the easiest route was also the most direct one in this case.

Anders stepped out onto the bridge, and he whispered words to connect to the currents of the air around him, dissipating some of the mist there. The gates before him were closed, huge and iron bound, with no obvious way to open them when they were locked shut. Soldiers in the red and purple of King Ravin stood before those gates, weapons ready to push back anyone who tried to get too close.

"Who goes there?" one called.

"My name is Anders Samis," Anders said, stepping forward toward the gates. "And I require entry to this castle."

"You *require* it?" the man shot back. "Well, our emperor requires that none enter, and he commands that northerners with weapons be taken or killed."

"Try," Anders said, drawing Loss in one smooth movement. The weapon felt so perfect, so *right* in his hands.

The soldier came forward at him, sword raised to strike. Ordinarily, Anders would have deflected the blow and then cut the man down. Now though, he let the attack come on, and then cut into it full force with his own weapon. He heard the ring of Loss as it struck, and the duller sound of the soldier's weapon as it shattered, fragments scattering around Anders.

Anders kicked the man then, sending him sprawling back to the cobbles. He turned to see another man coming for him and he stepped inside this blow, driving his shoulder into the man's chest. Instead of sweeping his blade up to cut his foe down as he gave ground, Anders kicked the soldier's legs out from under him.

Two of the guards had bows, and even as Anders watched they loosed arrows. Fortunately, Anders still had the vestiges of his connection to the air around him. He threw up a hand and stray gusts took the arrows, turning them aside from him as surely as a shield might have. Anders fed into that power, feeling where the wind wanted to go, building the storm until the localized force of it was enough to push back the men who came at him, making them struggle to even keep their feet.

He let the power fall, although in truth it wasn't something anyone could maintain for long. Such things needed a precise balance of forces, and even as trained as he was there was only so long Anders could cling to it. He didn't let the soldiers know that, though. Instead, he stood there, looking as if he might cut them all down at any moment. The only reason he hadn't so far was that it was always easier to talk to people when you hadn't killed those who served them.

Anders stood there and waited, leaning on his sword. He could hear shouting beyond the gates, and eventually, finally, the creak of a mechanism. The great gates started to swing open, and the guards found themselves caught between the need to get out of their way and the desire to keep clear of Anders's blade. Anders held his ground, letting them scurry around him.

A single man walked out, dressed in gilded armor. His dark beard was long and oiled, his eyes piercing as he looked at Anders. He was a large man, but more than that, there was a sense of dangerous strength within him as he approached. He held a two-handed blade, and Anders found himself wondering if he would swing it once he got close enough.

"Emperor Ravin," Anders said, with a bow that didn't take his eyes from the man there. "I wasn't sure if you would come out to do this yourself."

"You have caught my attention," the city's new ruler said. "Although that is a thing that can be as bad for someone as it could be good."

Anders knew that, knew exactly what kind of man he was dealing with. On another day, he wouldn't have wanted anything to do with a man like the emperor.

"You have attacked my men with magic," Ravin said.

"And yet they all still live," Anders pointed out. "If I wished to be your enemy, they would be dead."

Ravin nodded at that. He gestured to the mist. "And this? Is this magic too?"

"It is," Anders said. If Devin could claim his whole destiny, then Anders could at least claim the benefit of his workings. He pushed out another scrap of magic, clearing more of the mist around them.

"And the beast that attacked? The dragon? Was that you?" There was something coolly dangerous about Ravin's voice now.

Anders shook his head. "I fought against it. I have no love for such creatures."

The emperor thought for a few seconds. "What do you *want*, boy?"

"I want access to Master Grey's tower," Anders said. He didn't say all of it, not yet. He knew enough about the ways of royal courts to know that you didn't give away all that you wanted so early in a discussion. "I believe that I could make use of some of what lies within."

He saw Ravin looking him up and down. The emperor had a reputation as a clever man, one who saw the uses in all things. Anders was relying on that. It was why he had approached so openly.

"I might be able to provide such a thing," Ravin said. "To my own sorcerer."

Anders raised an eyebrow at that, as if he were surprised by it. "You're asking me to be your magus?"

"I'm told that a king needs such men," Ravin said. "And you clearly have skills. Who else could reward you as I could? If you want money, land, women ... I have them as no other man does. Serve me, and you will be rewarded. Refuse, and I cannot risk you being out in the world."

A dozen or more bowmen took up positions atop the walls. Anders knew a test when he saw one. Almost contemptuously, he blew them back from their positions, doing his best to hide the effort it took. He hid his joy at the offer, too. Not that he planned on serving a monster like this for long, but it was the best way to get what he actually wanted.

"Very well," he said. "But I have two conditions."

"Name them."

"First," he said. "I get everything in Master Grey's tower."

He saw the emperor nod. "And secondly?"

"If the old sorcerer returns, I want to be the one to kill him myself."

CHAPTER EIGHT

Shem had never been a man to listen to rumors. All thirty years of his life he'd worked this land, and he'd seen what was real and what wasn't. All his village was abuzz with this or that news of the invasion, or that an uprising was building, or that there were mysterious tales of magic coming out of some of the quiet places of the kingdom. Shem ignored all of it.

It was better just to stick to the work of his family's smallholding. His wife might like to talk about the fallen Knights of the Spur, or the efforts of Emperor Ravin's Quiet Men, or the rumors of flames in Astare, but none of that got the animals fed or the crops tended. Better to focus on simple, practical things. All that fancy stuff didn't affect them, not really.

Shem looked out at the village of Elloughton and sighed, wondering what market day would be like this time. Half the boys in the village had gone off to join this side or that, looking for adventure. It probably meant better prices for beets, but not much more than that.

He looked up at the sky, trying to guess at the weather. The weather typically meant more out here than all the wars of the world combined. Soldiers left places like this alone, but the rain coming or going, well, that could mean having food or starving, at a time like this.

For the first few moments, he only saw a speck against the clouds, big and dark, birdlike and yet not. For those seconds he didn't know *what* it was, and he could only stare at it, because it might be the most diversion he got all day out here.

Then the shape resolved itself, and a kind of disbelieving terror rose up inside Shem. It was an old terror, born out of stories and deeper things, something inside him telling him that this shape, this sight, meant danger.

He ran for his house as the dragon swooped in, huge and black and dangerous. It came down toward the village, and dark flames billowed from its mouth, rippling toward the village. Below it, people started to scream. Shem joined his voice to theirs, shouting for his wife and his son, even as the creature wheeled around.

"Tasha! Ben! Get out of the house!"

Even as he called out, the dragon passed by again, flames pouring down to consume the tiny house they called home. Shem screamed his anguish as he saw it, feeling the heat of the flames close by, his grief and his terror urging him to fling himself forward into those flames to try to get to those he loved. The heat was too great, though, pushing him back, forcing him to stand there in the field before his holding while flames and smoke consumed everything.

Around him, smoke seemed to fill the world, blocking off everything other than the lines of fire that stood where the village had been just moments before. Those flames licked up, weirdly shadowed around the edges, both bright and dark at the same time.

Shem choked on the smoke, feeling it deep in his lungs, blocking out most of the sky above. He couldn't tell where he was in it, had to establish the world around him by the cries of fear and the roar of the fire. In the chaos of it all, Shem could hear the screams of those caught in the flames, the terror of the dying. He couldn't see the dragon now, but the terror he felt deep inside him told him that it was still up there somewhere.

He stood there, hands out, trying to work out where he was. The smoke billowed and shifted, distorting the world around him. Through it, Shem could barely make out the outlines of the houses.

There was something else, too, coming through the smoke. For the first few moments, Shem thought that the shape was something human, a woman staggering to safety, but as it grew closer, he saw the claws on the hands, the scales covering its flesh. The creature stood as tall as most men would have, iridescent blue scales covering it from head to foot. It wore a kind of robe over those scales, and strangely intelligent eyes looked out of a face that seemed caught somewhere between reptilian and human.

He stood there in terror as the creature approached, sure that he was about to be torn limb from limb. He wanted to run, but couldn't.

Instead, the creature stopped in front of him, placing one clawed hand on his throat to hold him in place. Shem shook with fear, not knowing if he should fight, or try to flee, or just faint from the horror of it all.

"You will be the one who goes out into the world," she said, in a voice that sounded surprisingly normal, for all that she looked strange. "You will tell people about the destruction here. Tell them that Princess Nerra is responsible. Tell them that she is Perfected, and that the dragon-kin are coming for them. Tell them that more will burn."

She shoved Shem away from her, and he stumbled, staring at her, not knowing what to do.

"Run, human-thing," she said. "*Run.*"

He did. He ran, and as the screams continued behind him, he didn't dare to look back.

⚜ ⚜ ⚜

Nerra remounted Shadr, and the dragon queen propelled them back into the sky. Shadr powered up through the smoke, out into the clear blue beyond, and Nerra drew in a cooling breath. Her senses were so sharp that she could taste the blood and the smoke on the air, the fear and the death.

Will the one you spoke to do what is required? Shadr asked through the connection between them.

"He will tell others what he saw," Nerra assured her. "He will tell them about you."

And about her. He would tell those he met what he had seen, and what she had said to him. He would remember the touch of her clawed hand on his skin, and her voice as she had told him who she was.

We still need to burn more, Shadr insisted.

Nerra understood that. From the moment Alith had returned to them, telling them about the amulet, this had been necessary.

Do not think about that one, Shadr instructed her. *She is nothing compared to the power we have together.*

Nerra was a little surprised by that. "You sound almost...jealous."

I am not jealous, Shadr replied. The great black dragon wheeled above the burning village below. *But you are my chosen. We belong together, and the one you merely found has no part of it.*

"I'm not about to go to Alith," Nerra said. "She was merely the one to tell us about the amulet."

The amulet must be found and destroyed.

Nerra could feel the determination in Shadr, but also the hint of fear underneath that response. Nerra could understand that, because she'd seen some of the horrors that had come when the human-things had used the amulet in their rebellion against dragon kind, so long ago.

She'd seen the dragons controlled, forced to kill others of their kind. She'd seen the ones driven from the air so that human-things could strike at them with their weapons. Nerra had seen horror after horror, with precious dragon lives wasted by these creatures that seemed to infest the world.

A small, distant part of Nerra reminded her that once she had been one of the human-things, yet it didn't feel like it now. She was so much *more* than they were now, so much more than they could ever be. Even the animal Lesser, who were not Perfected as she was, were still faster and stronger than humans, closer to the true beauty of the dragons.

She thought of those who had died when Shadr struck at the village. It wasn't that she had no sympathy for them, no wish that this could be done without deaths. It was simply that if it came to a choice between the deaths of dragons at the hands of human-things holding the amulet and the deaths of a few of those humans, there was no choice to be made.

It will be more than a few, before this is done, Shadr sent to her with relish. *Our army will sweep down, once the way is clear.*

For now, though, there was the question of the amulet. Nerra had guessed wrong in saying that it might be in Astare. Now the city lay largely in ashes, and there was no sign of the amulet. It had been in Royalsport all along, which meant that it was too close to dangerous hands that might be able to use it to its full, devastating potential.

They needed to lure out the one who carried it, and that meant the stench of burning flesh, carried on the wind. It meant Shadr and Nerra striking away from their army, and individual dragons sent to inflict terror. It meant a line of burning across the land that their foes would not be able to ignore.

Where next? Shadr asked. Nerra knew that the dragon queen was relying on her to pick the points that would hurt the human-things most. This village had always supplied food for the royal armies, so it made sense that burning it would get a reaction.

Nerra thought of more villages, more targets. They could destroy a waystation inn, perhaps, guaranteed to be filled with travelers who might deliver news. Alternatively, they could hit another farm, or perhaps a military outpost... anything that would draw out their foes.

That was a part of why she had told the human who she was, reasoning that the name might draw even more attention than just the fire and the death. Those who had the amulet would presumably know enough about dragons to know about the Perfected, and the sight of her there would help to lend credence to the story.

Even so, Nerra was a little worried about revealing her name like that. What if it brought trouble that they did not expect? What if she had done the wrong thing again, and this time it put them in more danger?

I will keep us safe, Shadr promised. *I will keep all our kin safe.*

There was such certainty attached to the words that appeared in Nerra's mind that it was hard to keep her own doubts in the face of them. She knew that Shadr would do everything she could to keep her safe. Nerra was more worried about her own part in this. She had to protect dragon-kind, had to find and destroy the amulet.

And that meant that they weren't done. Plenty more villages still had to burn.

Chapter Nine

R enard led Erin through the still burning city, picking out a route for them that would take them to the walls. He led the way over the streams, blending in with the strings of people who were running this way and that, trying to save their homes and those of others.

To Renard's surprise, there were relatively few looters in the chaos. Oh, there were a few, because there always were at times like this, but to his practiced eye they had the look of amateurs rather than real experts, picking through the bones of a house in hope rather than breaking in where they knew they would find rich pickings.

"So we get to the gates, kill the guards, and then what?" the princess asked.

"You know," Renard said, "for someone so short, you're remarkably bloodthirsty."

She glared up at him. "Are you going to tell me that you have something against killing southern soldiers?"

Renard shrugged. "I've killed my share of men when I've been stealing, but when I do, it usually means that things have gone wrong on the job."

"And do things go wrong for you a lot?" Erin demanded as Renard chose between two streets, trying to find the most secluded route to the wall that he could.

"Hardly ever," Renard assured her. "The gods love me."

He'd always been a good liar, and this didn't seem like a thing where the truth would be all that helpful. Thankfully, before the princess could ask any questions, one of the gates loomed ahead of them. There were half a dozen guards on it; more than usual, perhaps in response to the chaos.

Renard resisted the urge to swear, because it didn't seem like the thing to do in front of a princess. Erin, however, spat a mouthful of invective that would suit any sailor. She also hefted her spear.

"Don't be hasty," Renard said. "All we need is—"

"What?" Erin demanded in return.

That was the moment the mist rose, seeming to burst up from the fires around them. It was thick, and soupy, and impossible, seeming to come from nowhere to douse the fires, and leaving the world coated in a thick fog that meant Renard could barely see his hand in front of his face. Renard heard the guards at the gate exclaim in shock and start forward, as if trying to work out what was going on.

"As I was saying, all we need is a suitable distraction," Renard said with a smile. "I *told* you that the gods loved me."

He put a finger to his lips, and Erin followed in his wake on surprisingly silent feet. There was an art to sneaking among a crowd of people, and to Renard's surprise, the princess proved surprisingly adept at it, slipping by shadows in the mist while they were still trying to work out why that mist was there at all. Renard was just as curious, but if he'd learned anything by this point in his life it was not to let curiosity get in the way of a good escape.

They were almost through when the mist cleared just enough for one of the guards to be left staring at them.

"Who—" the man began, and Renard kicked him back without hesitating.

"Run!" he yelled to Erin, all but dragging her along in his wake as they sprinted for safety. Renard pulled the princess through the slums of the outer city, not stopping until the sounds of pursuit faded into the background.

He kept going until his lungs burned with the effort, and Renard was a little surprised by how long that was. It seemed that he was recovering well now that he didn't have the amulet anymore. He felt a little guilty about leaving it in the rubble of the noble quarter, but for now the priority had to be getting the princess to safety. *Especially* when dragons might arrive at any moment if anyone found it. Renard had no wish to be around for more of those.

"I thought you said you were lucky," Erin demanded, as they slowed to a walk.

Renard shrugged. "We're still alive, aren't we? Now, we need to steal horses."

Of course, out in the outer city, decent horses were hard to find, and in any case, many had been spooked by the dragon's attack. Still, he found one broad-shouldered pony tied to a cart in front of what seemed to be a brewer's yard. To a man like Renard, it was practically an invitation.

An hour later, they were driving their stolen wagon slowly along the road out of Royalsport and into the woods. Very slowly, as it happened, because it turned out that the dray horse only understood the notion of moving at one speed: a carefully sustained walk. The thing seemed stubborn too; it was all Renard could do to keep it headed out into the countryside, rather than going off about its usual route around Royalsport's taverns.

"This isn't really the quick getaway I had in mind," Erin said, as Renard gently flicked the reins to keep the creature moving. They were entering the forest that lay well beyond Royalsport now, the trees arching overhead. "Honestly, I think we could *walk* faster than this."

"But this is more comfortable," Renard pointed out. "Trust me, there are plenty of worse ways to make an escape. As I recall, the *last* time I left the House of Sighs, I ended up running with no shoes, and with half a dozen men chasing me."

"Did you fight *those*?" Erin asked.

Renard shrugged. "Fighting is overrated. I mean, if you *have* to kill a man, then by all means; there's no one who can deny my fame as a swordsman."

"*I've* never heard of you," Erin pointed out.

"But that's just because my skill as a thief means it never comes up," Renard said. "Honest, mostly... I'd rather drink."

To prove his point, he reached back for one of the barrels of ale on the cart. To his annoyance, he saw that it was split and empty. No wonder the brewer had just abandoned the cart. Worse, since it had presumably happened in the dragon attack, it probably counted as Renard's fault.

"Oh, all right," he said, hopping down from the cart. "Maybe walking *will* be faster."

He cut the horse free from its stays. The creature seemed to consider its newfound freedom for a moment, then trotted back vaguely in the direction of Royalsport. Renard sighed at that. There was probably a metaphor for his existence in all this somewhere. He trudged on into the forest with Erin by his side.

They walked, and walked, hours passing them by, the sun moving slowly across the sky. For the most part, they walked in silence, watching out for dangers. At one point Renard started to sing just to relieve the boredom, and Erin stopped him with a look.

He sighed. "I get that reaction a lot."

They kept going.

"So," Erin asked, after they'd been walking for what seemed like forever. "Why did Lady Meredith of the House of Sighs kiss you as you left?"

"Well," Renard said, "things are … complicated between us."

"How complicated?" Erin asked. She was obviously looking for something to pass the time as they walked, and Renard was grateful for it too. He'd never been a man to abide silences except where he needed them to avoid danger.

"Well," he said. "She and I were once …" He tried to think of the right words for what they'd been. "I suppose you could say that we were in love."

"You suppose?" Erin countered. "Don't you know?"

"As I say," Renard said, "it's complicated."

"What did you do?" Erin asked.

That seemed a little harsh. After all, he'd saved her life, and she'd really only known him a short while.

"There may or may not have been one or two betrayals between us," Renard admitted. "And a theft from one of the House of Sighs' more lucrative patrons, and of course a small riot, and …"

"Shh!" Erin hissed.

"I thought you would want to hear the story," Renard said. "Or am I—"

"Shh! Listen!"

Renard listened, and heard the unmistakable sound of feet tracking them through the woodland. He gestured to Erin and slipped from the path, moving silently, using the trees for cover. He heard the sound of the footsteps growing closer, but then they stopped. He turned toward Erin.

"You've spooked them," he said, but she wasn't there. The space beside Renard stood empty.

That emptiness didn't last long. A man in the dun clothes of a forester stepped out in front of Renard, a long knife in his hand. Renard started to edge his own hand toward a blade, but the man in front of him shook his head.

"Best not to unless you want to be cut down, friend," the man said. He had the look of a thief to him now that Renard was looking closer, or perhaps a soldier. Not that there was ever much difference to tell between the two, in Renard's experience.

Renard sighed. "If this is a robbery, then I have to say that I have depressingly little for you."

"Who are you?" the man demanded. "What are you doing here?"

Renard struggled to think of a suitable lie, which wasn't really like him at all. Somehow, though, he doubted that this man would believe that he'd just been out for a nice stroll in the forest, or that he was there to deliver a message.

"Well?" the man demanded.

That was when Erin struck. She moved with the grace of a leaping cat, jumping from the branches of a nearby tree that she must have climbed in almost perfect silence. The impact of her fall knocked down the man and she rose up over him, her spear poised to strike. Renard braced himself for the moment when that spear would come down and finish things.

Yet even as Renard watched, she held back, not plunging that spear home in its target.

"Wait," Erin said. "I ... I know you."

The man might have answered, but it seemed that Erin had knocked the breath from him.

"I *trained* you," Erin said. "Or I started to. You're one of the men who came to join my sister's army."

The man wheezed, but managed to nod. Renard took that as his cue to help the man back to his feet. It was several seconds before the man was able to speak.

"Where's my sister?" Erin said. "What are you doing out here, away from the farm?"

Finally, the man managed to force out words.

"F ... follow me ... princess."

Chapter Ten

O dd was restless as he stood in the command tent, candles flicking around him now as the light was starting to fail. He had his hands on the table that held their maps, and he could feel the twitchiness in his fingers, urging him to sweep them all to the floor that had been created from rugs and old sheets. They'd spent most of the day marching closer to Royalsport, but now, Odd was about ready to stalk out and head back in the direction they'd come.

Restlessness was *not* a good thing for him; too close to all the old angers he'd pushed down, too far from the beautiful stillness he'd learned to find at the heart of the fight. It turned out that, while he could meditate happily while a sword was coming at his head, poring over plans left him short-tempered.

"I'm telling you, that approach would get our troops cut down in minutes!" he snapped at the prince. He caught Lenore's expression. "I'm sorry, my queen."

"I know you're frustrated," Lenore said, "but we can find a way to do this. We have to."

Odd could feel the trust behind those words, but also the pressure that came with that trust. It meant that that life after life, potentially the fate of the entire kingdom, lay in his hands. It was so much easier when all he had to worry about was wading into the enemy, killing those in front of him, caught up in the flow of it all.

He, Lenore, and Greave had been discussing strategy for what seemed like hours now, and it wasn't going well. It wasn't that he lacked tactical knowledge: he'd attacked his share of forts and settlements. The prince, meanwhile, was full of ideas, drawn from battles and wars Odd had barely even heard of. Currently, he was sketching out a kind of covered battering ram that would withstand boiling oil, trying to work out a way that it could be built from nothing but the trees around them.

Lenore was providing her own ideas, but mostly she seemed to be serving as an intermediary, reining in Greave's most elaborate schemes, reminding Odd that not everyone could fight like him. She seemed able to bear in mind the nature and skills of their troops better than either of them, every inch their queen.

They were still trying to find a way to assault Royalsport when three figures came into the broad tent they were working within. Odd recognized one as a man he'd sent out to scout for dangers, making sure that Ravin's army didn't become aware of them before they were ready to strike. The others...

Lenore was already throwing herself forward at her sister, sweeping her up in a hug that looked as if it might crush her.

"You're alive! You're safe," she said. "Erin, I was so worried. What happened? You're injured!"

"I'm fine," Erin insisted.

Prince Greave was standing there by the side of them, and as Lenore finally let go of her sister, he was there to take her place, hugging her as tightly as Lenore had.

"I thought you were dead!" Erin said.

"From what I heard, I was just as worried about you," Greave replied. "You really went to try to kill Ravin?"

"I didn't succeed," Erin said. She looked embarrassed, even ashamed at the failure.

"The main thing is that you're safe," Greave said.

When he pulled back, it was Odd's turn, but Erin already looked embarrassed at being hugged so much, and Odd wasn't the kind of person who had ever hugged anyone. The most he could do was reach out a hand to clasp hers, forearm to forearm, the way a warrior would.

He wanted to say so much in that moment. He wanted to apologize for the ways in which he'd pushed her to be more, wanted to explain that he'd just been trying to keep her safe. He wanted to let her know that he understood what it was like to live with so much anger, and not to be able to do anything about it.

"I...I'm glad you're not dead," he managed. "Do your injuries hurt much?"

He cursed himself for not being able to say any of what he actually meant. He'd never been good at apologies, maybe because he'd never been able to find any large enough to cover some of the things he'd done. He wanted to ask Erin if she could ever forgive him for pulling her away during the death of her mother, if she understood that he only had her safety in mind. He couldn't find the words for any of that.

"I'm...it's okay," Erin replied, her grip just as tight as Odd's.

"Eloquent," the other man there said, with a slight smirk. He was broad-shouldered and red-haired, looking like he could fight, but also looking round as if he was expecting trouble at any moment.

"Who is this?" Odd asked Erin, grateful for the chance to talk about something, anything, else.

"This is Renard," she said. "He's a thief who helped to get me out of the city."

"Then I'm grateful to you," Odd said.

"We all are," Lenore agreed. "I am Queen Lenore. This is my brother Greave, and this is my general, Sir Odd."

Odd moved forward to clasp the other man's hand almost as he had Erin's. He was glad that this man had brought Erin back to them. At the same time, Odd felt a thread of worry running through him. He thought back to stories of a big, red-haired thief, and of some of the chaos that had followed in his wake.

"I've heard of you," Odd said, carefully.

"And I have heard of you," Renard replied. "I've sung the *Ballad of the Mad Knight* enough times."

Odd had heard it. Being reminded of it didn't improve his mood.

"Renard isn't just here to bring me back," Erin said, perhaps sensing some of the tension in that moment. "He's come bearing information from the city."

"Information from a thief?" Odd said.

"I've been in the House of Sighs," Renard said. He seemed to realize how that sounded. "Lady Meredith has been trying to coordinate between people who stand in opposition to the emperor." He turned to Lenore. "Your maid Orianne is a part of it, my queen."

"She's safe?" Lenore said, sounding relieved.

Renard nodded. He turned to Prince Greave. "Aurelle is there too."

Odd saw the prince swallow, although he didn't say anything. He looked as if he was trying to contain a whole swirl of emotions in that moment, and Odd couldn't begin to guess at any of them.

"That's … good to know," the prince said, although he didn't sound as if he knew whether it was good or not.

"Is that your news?" Odd asked. "That a few people we know are still alive? Why should we even trust that, when you're a thief?"

"He's all right, Odd," Erin said. "He saved me, and … I think he can be trusted. Besides, I've heard most of this myself, from Meredith and the others. Please, just … trust me."

"I do," Odd said. He saw Erin relax a little at that, as if she'd been holding her breath, expecting a different answer.

"And Renard," Erin said, "Odd isn't the man you think he is. He isn't the man he *was*, either."

It was probably the closest thing the two of them were ever going to get to an apology, and all because of the thief. Odd relaxed a little. If Erin was prepared to trust this man, maybe he should as well.

"Actually," Renard said, "I'm here to say that we've been making preparations within the city. Aurelle has been working on some of Ravin's noble allies, trying to get them to split from his cause. Orianne has been finding allies in the city. Meredith has found a way into the castle itself. When the attack comes, they'll be ready."

Odd considered that for a moment or two. "Most of those who would rise up willingly have already fallen."

He could see the pain on Lenore's and Erin's faces as he said it, but it *did* need to be said.

The thief shrugged in response. "I know what some of these people can be like. Think a thief will betray you? We have to have enough trust to work with each other again. A noble … if they think there's something in it for them, they'll move to pick the winning side. It's how they got to where they are."

"Which means that they will only do it if we can convince them that they *are* on the winning side," Lenore said, sounding thoughtful.

Odd found himself thinking of their journey to Lord Carrick's holdings, and how quickly the nobleman had been willing to betray them to further his position. He'd been sure that they couldn't win, and so he'd wanted to get what he could from the situation, rather than helping Lenore with something that wasn't already a certainty.

At the same time, he'd seen the way that Lenore had been able to convince his men to her side, and so many others, including nobles. If anyone could convince the ones still in the city to fight at their side, it was Lenore, but even for her, Odd suspected that she would need to make it clear that she could win. Even if they did change sides, Odd knew that it still wouldn't be simple.

"Ravin will be ready for an uprising," he said. "And he'll be waiting for any attack we make on the walls."

"He's been ready for every move that we've made," Lenore agreed with him. She paced the tent, not looking happy. "That's been the problem. It has felt like he's been setting things up from the start, knowing exactly how we'll all react."

Greave chose that moment to speak up. "Then we have to be the ones to work out how *he'll* react. Doesn't van Halt write that 'knowledge of the enemy's likely responses is an advantage in all warfare'?"

"I don't know, does he?" Odd replied. He hadn't read as many books as the prince, but even so, the sentiment seemed like a valid one.

"He does," Greave said. He was staring down at the map now, moving his fingers from this point to that. "And I've seen how he works. This reminds me of something…"

"What?" Lenore asked.

"The siege of Yantrin," Greave replied, looking triumphant, as if those words explained everything. "It's just like the siege of Yantrin, three centuries ago."

Odd frowned at him, although, to be fair, so did everyone else there.

"You're going to have to explain," he said.

He did, and as he started to do so, Odd started to feel hope. For the first time, he couldn't instantly see the practical problems in the plan. For the first time, it seemed as if they might actually have a chance.

"It's dangerous," he said, looking over to Lenore. "But it might work."

For her part, the queen seemed determined. She nodded once, gravely and slowly. "It's the best chance we have. Give the men their orders. We will need to march tonight to be in position. We attack tomorrow at dawn."

CHAPTER ELEVEN

G reave couldn't sleep that night, so he sat up, staring at the stars, watching their movements as he had so many times in his life. Once, he would have noted their positions and their movements, checking them against the observations of the finest minds the House of Scholars had produced.

Now, he just stared, hoping. He'd been the one to come up with the idea for what was to follow, he'd helped to plan the things that would come next. There was nothing left to do but sleep, and yet he couldn't. The camp around him was mostly dark and silent, but there were still fires here and there, marking the spots where groups of soldiers sat, waiting. Greave didn't go to any of those fires. Instead, he sat there in the darkness on the edge of the camp, alone except for his thoughts.

There were more than enough of those to go around. What if he'd gotten this wrong? What if he'd misjudged the plan, or misjudged Ravin? The others had agreed so readily when Greave had set out his plan, but maybe that was just because they didn't know all the facts. He'd told them about the siege of Yantrin, but not about Hannard Point a year later, when the same tactic had led to ruin.

Greave looked out in the direction where he knew Royalsport lay. He thought about the walls of the city, solid and stone built. He thought about the walls of the castle within, and the keep inside even that. As a child, those walls had always seemed so impenetrable, such a feat of engineering that it barely seemed conceivable that they'd been raised by human hands. Even when he'd read the accounts of their building, he'd marveled at the skills of those who had built them, and the ability to get so many men and women to come together for one common cause. The work that had been put into them only made them seem stronger, and now his plan was supposed to let them achieve victory in the face of those walls?

Another thought came to Greave, hot on the heels of the others: Aurelle was in there somewhere. He'd thought...he'd been *certain* that she was gone, and yet she was there, in the midst of the buildings and the lights, somewhere. He didn't know what to think about that, what to *feel*. It all still felt so complicated when it came to her, and yet so simple, all at the same time. The moment Renard had mentioned her name, he'd wanted to shake the other man, demanding to know more. He'd known that he couldn't, though; this moment, this battle to come, was the focus now.

As for what he might say to her, he was still thinking about that when a shadow came up out of the darkness to sit down beside him, settling into place and watching the city.

"You couldn't sleep either?" Greave asked as Lenore took the spot beside him.

She shook her head.

"Look around, Greave," she said softly. "There are so many people, all relying on me to get this right. In the morning, I'm going to command them to go into battle, and...how many of them will die?"

"Some of them will," Greave admitted. He looked around at the shadowy forms of the men and women of their army. It seemed that plenty of them couldn't sleep either. "Perhaps a lot of them."

Perhaps *all* of them if he'd judged this wrong.

"The plan will work though," Lenore said. "If the nobles in the city are convinced to do their part, I believe it will succeed. You're right about Ravin, and the way he will act."

"I hope so," Greave said. "And that this isn't all another trap where he's yet another step ahead."

Lenore shook her head. "Not this time. This time, we'll win. We have to."

Greave smiled across at her. "You know that you don't have to convince me? It's all right to be nervous, here and now."

"Good," Lenore replied, "because I'm terrified."

They sat there like that in the dark together, staring out into the forest. Greave wasn't entirely surprised when a third figure slid into place next to them. Erin had her spear across her knees. It was obvious that, whatever wounds she'd suffered in the city, she planned to join the fight tomorrow.

"I'm surprised that Odd isn't here," Erin said.

"The last I saw of him, he was sleeping," Lenore replied. "Apparently battle nerves aren't so much of a thing for him."

"Probably just for anyone about to face him," Greave said. He'd read the stories of Sir Oderick. This man didn't seem quite like everything those stories said, but there was still something dangerous about him. "Is he as deadly as they say?"

"More," Erin said.

"Which is exactly what we need," Lenore pointed out.

"It's probably just as well he's not here," Erin said. She passed what proved to be a wineskin over to Greave. "Three of us sitting here staring at nothing is probably enough."

They sat there in silence for a while. Briefly, Greave reflected that there had been few enough times when they'd been together like this. When they'd been younger, Erin had always wanted to be off having adventures in the grounds of the castle, or the city, or the lands beyond. Lenore had always been at court, trying to live up to the standards that her mother set for her as a princess, and as for Greave, he'd usually been in the library. They'd spent less time together than they should have, but they were together here, now, for this.

"I wish Nerra were here, too," Greave said. He'd traveled so far to try to find a cure for her, and now that he had it, she wasn't there to take it. Briefly, he wondered if he should tell his sisters that he'd found that cure, but no, this wasn't the moment to distract them. He would explain it *after* the battle.

"With a battle coming, I think I'd rather have Rodry," Erin said.

"I wish they were both here," Lenore said.

None of them openly wished for Vars's presence, and Greave felt a moment of sadness at that. The greater sadness, though, was for the ways in which his family had fallen apart.

He found himself wishing that things could be as they had been before all this, with their family safe, and together. Yet he realized that there were things about that past that he wouldn't want to go back to. He wouldn't want to go back to his brothers and his father thinking that he was useless because he had his head buried in a book most of the time. He wouldn't want to go back to a time when Nerra had been forced to hide her illness, terrified of what would happen if she didn't, where Erin had found herself forced to run away, and Lenore had the full weight of her mother's interference, trying to make her into a perfect princess.

"What are you thinking?" Lenore asked Greave, obviously noting his thoughtful look.

"Just that we've come a long way," Greave said.

"Literally, in your case," Lenore pointed out. "I always thought you'd be content to stay in the castle library, but you've traveled further than any of us."

That was true. He'd traveled around the kingdom, and beyond. He'd seen more danger than he'd ever expected. He was a very different man as a result. He'd willingly stepped into danger, had survived in the wilds, had even killed. He could remember the gentle, bookish boy he'd been, but he wasn't that boy anymore.

"You've both come a long way yourselves," Greave said. "I never thought when I came back that I would find one of my sisters a queen and the other a warrior."

He hadn't thought that he would see them again at all.

"I never thought it would be like this to fight," Erin said. "It's so different from playing soldiers with Rodry. It's different even from when I was training with Master Wendros."

"It's very different when there's your life on the line," Greave said, and Erin gave him a thoughtful look. He hadn't told her about the man he'd killed, but he could see from the look on her face that she knew.

"It's hard when there's *anyone's* life on the line," Lenore said. That was the difference between them. Greave might have tried to protect Aurelle, and might have traveled to try to save Nerra, but he'd never truly had people relying on him.

Except now. It was his plan that they would be following, after all, yet still, that was nothing compared to the pressures that Lenore probably felt.

As they sat there, looking more ragged and bruised than they ever would have at court, Greave could see that even as his sisters had changed so much, they'd also become exactly who they'd always been meant to be. Erin had always had it in her to fight, and now it seemed that she had become a warrior to be feared, her determination matched by a new understanding of the dangers of the world. Lenore had always been noble and kind, loving and elegant, but now it seemed that she had steel running beneath it too.

"What will you do after all this?" Erin asked.

Greave wasn't sure that he could imagine an after to all of this. "I need to finish…" again, he didn't want to distract Erin with thoughts of the cure "…what I went to do, and Aurelle…" He shook his head. "If I don't survive all this—"

"Don't talk like that," Erin said. "It's bad luck before a battle. If you think about death too much, you attract it."

Greave had seen death come to plenty of people who hadn't even seen it coming, but for now, he went along with his sister. She was the expert, after all.

There was probably so much else they could have said then, so many other things that he wished he *could* say to them. This didn't feel like a time for words anymore, though. In that moment, all that was left was to sit there, thinking of all the ones who hadn't lived long enough to see this moment, and all the things that might follow.

Greave sat there with his sisters, waiting for the sun to come up, and for battle to come to Royalsport. Right then, there was nowhere else he would rather have been.

CHAPTER TWELVE

A s dawn broke over the camp, Lenore set her heels to her horse. This
was the moment; this was the beginning. The horse started forward,
and around her, her army moved.

Men and women followed in her wake, soldiers of Lord Ness, Lord
Renslipp, and Lord Welles, ordinary peasant folk, former soldiers of her
father, and more. They advanced slowly through the trees, saving their
energy for what they knew was going to come.

Odd rode beside her, still wearing his makeshift robes over his armor,
his sword by his side. Erin rode at her other side, her spear ready and a
small shield strapped to her arm. Greave was next to her. From somewhere, he'd found a chain shirt, a partial helm, and a slender sword that
looked more suited to being worn at court than to the rigors of a battle.
Renard was not there, because that wasn't the task Lenore had given him.

In that moment, Lenore knew that as much as Greave had helped to
plan what was going to happen, he didn't belong on the front lines of a
battle. She couldn't imagine him wading into the fray, trying to cut down
his foes.

"Greave," she said as they rode, "when the fighting starts, I want you
to position yourself at the rear of the army."

"You don't want me to help with the fighting?" Greave asked.

"I think that's the best spot for you to help," Lenore replied. "You've
come up with the plan for this, planning is what you do best. Your eyes
and your mind are more useful than your sword arm in this, brother."

"I..." Greave hesitated, and then nodded. "Illius says that a man
should know his own limits, and that stretching beyond them only causes
failure."

"Let us hope that none of us is stretching beyond our limits here," Lenore said. She turned to Erin, for what she knew would be the harder conversation to have. Her sister was already shaking her head.

"No," Erin said. "I'll not stay back like some kind of child."

"Not like a child," Lenore said. "Like someone who's *injured.* Don't think I haven't seen you limping around the camp. Besides, do you think that half the enemy forces won't try to converge wherever you are?"

Erin still didn't look happy about it, but then, Lenore hadn't really expected her to. She tried to think of a way to persuade her, knowing how badly simply telling her what to do had gone in the past.

"Besides, this way I'll know that Greave has someone to protect him," Lenore said. "I need you to do this, Erin. Please."

Even then, her sister hesitated. Finally, she nodded.

"All right, I'll do it," she said. She pulled away a little, but she didn't go to the back yet. She was obviously going to leave it as long as possible before she went, if she went at all. Greave stayed with her, and he smiled over at Lenore. He knew what Lenore had done. Lenore just hoped that all their plans worked so well today.

She hoped that *this* plan worked. Her sister had gone off and done her own thing a couple of times now, and it was obvious that she didn't like the idea of being pushed to the back of things. Lenore didn't care; she just wanted her sister to be safe. She didn't want to come through all of this, only to find that Erin had been cut down in some unknown corner of the battlefield.

"You know that she will not follow your command?" Odd said beside Lenore.

"I have to hope," Lenore said.

"Are you sure that *you* won't go to the back?" Odd asked her. "The dangers that you have described for your sister are just as great for you. Every soldier Ravin has will come for you, my queen."

"I know," Lenore said. She'd felt what it was like to be at the heart of a battle, back in the battle for the bridge, what seemed like an eternity ago now. She'd seen the chaos of it all, heard the screams of the dying and the fury of men trying to kill one another almost mindlessly. She didn't want to be there in the middle of another battle, but she knew that there wasn't any other option.

"You're not going, are you?" Odd asked.

"I need to be there, Odd," Lenore said. "The plan doesn't work without me. More than that, so many people are only here because I convinced them. If I hang back, hide, stay safe, do you think they'll willingly risk their lives?"

She heard Odd sigh. "I know. I just wish that there were a less dangerous way to do this."

Lenore wished it too, but no one had ever said that retaking a kingdom would be easy. She forced herself to look confident as her forces headed out from the trees, across the fields and the open ground that led toward the city.

Its walls rose in the distance, smoke coming from behind them, and to Lenore's eye, not all of it could be put down to the work of the House of Weapons or the kilns. Houses spread out in front of the walls, and many of them were damaged or destroyed. Lenore could see people going about their business there in the streets of the slums outside the walls, their houses wood rather than stone, pressed together tightly.

They ran for cover within their houses as Lenore's army approached. Lenore couldn't blame them; they'd already seen what it could be like when an army invaded a city. Just because the city was Lenore's by right, that didn't mean that a battle to retake it wouldn't ravage it, and threaten the lives of the people who lived within it.

That was why they'd come up with the plan that they had. Lenore rode out onto the open ground before the city, and her army arranged itself in lines and wedges, the disposition determined before they'd even left. Troops that Lord Welles had provided sat on the left flank, while others from Lords Renslipp and Ness formed up on the right. Peasant fighters and bandits took the centerground, the idea being that if an enemy tried to strike at those who seemed weakest, the flanks would be able to close around to encircle them.

The very last of the line brought some of the things Greave had designed with them, covered rams and palisades, frames that might let them build catapults and the beginnings of ballistae. They started to set them out in front of the city as Lenore signaled for the rest of them to hold their ground.

Slowly, deliberately, she rode forward with Odd by her side, along with Erin and Greave. She lifted a lance as she passed a stack of them, then kept going. Together, they rode through the poorer parts of the city, and there were cheers here and there as she passed, some of them obviously recognizing who she was. For the most part, though, it was silent, with people either scared of what might follow, or worried about what it might mean if a Quiet Man heard them.

The gates to the city were closing as Lenore approached, and she didn't bother approaching closer. Certainly, she wasn't going to get within bow shot when she knew that Ravin's troops wouldn't hesitate. Instead, she drew her horse to a halt, jamming the lance she carried into the ground.

She reached back on the saddle for a rolled length of cloth, unfurling it to reveal a flag. It was in the blue and gold of her family, but the design was her own: a single white hart wearing a golden crown.

She attached it to the lance, so that it stood there fluttering in the breeze. She sat atop her horse, unmoving now, just waiting. Around Lenore, she could see people moving in the buildings of Royalsport's outer areas, and she could see the way that Erin and Odd both looked around sharply, watching out for any threat. Lenore trusted them, but also trusted the people of her city. *They* weren't the ones who were going to try to kill her.

She waited, and waited, until finally the gates stopped closing long enough to allow a single figure out, dressed in the red and purple of one of Ravin's soldiers. The man made his way forward, looking nervous as he came. As he got closer, Lenore saw that he wasn't even an officer, just an ordinary soldier, armored in a chain shirt and carrying a curving sword. She didn't move to meet him, just waited the minutes it took to make his way through the city's streets to her.

"What's the meaning of this?" he demanded. He reached for the banner Lenore had set out, then stopped short as Erin's spear all but appeared before him, making it clear what would happen if he touched it.

Lenore took a breath, looking down at the man. She almost felt sorry for him, since he was going to have to convey her words to Emperor Ravin.

"I am Lenore, daughter of Godwin the Third and Queen Aethe. I stand here with my sister Erin and my brother Greave. I am the rightful queen of this land, and I mean to take it back from the invader, Ravin."

The guard looked like he didn't know what to say to that. That was fine; Lenore just kept going.

"If necessary, I will take Royalsport one street at a time," she said. She gestured to the spot where her siege machines stood, people clustering around them. "But the truth is that I have no wish to destroy the city even while I take it. So instead, I invite King Ravin to meet my army upon the field of battle."

"Army?" the guardsman said, with a snort. "You call *that* an army?"

Lenore caught Erin's move to strike in time, stopping her with a gesture.

"Erin, enough." She waited until Erin lowered her spear before she continued. "I know how few people I have," she said. "But they are fighting for their homes, fighting for what *matters*. Tell King Ravin that when you see him. Tell him to meet me out there, if he dares."

The guard stood there for a moment or two, just staring.

"Go!" Lenore ordered him, and he all but ran for the safety of the gate once more.

She waited until he reached it, then turned and rode back toward her own lines. Soon, it would begin. She just hoped that she'd judged this right.

CHAPTER THIRTEEN

R avin dressed carefully, slowly, picking out his clothes with the care that he might have taken picking out armor. He took a robe of deepest purple and put it on over a white tunic and blood red britches. He weighed his crown in his hands, setting it on his brow carefully, looking at himself and making sure he conveyed the image he wanted to convey.

When the dragon had been raging, he had been a man protecting what was his, shut away in the castle. Now, he needed to look magnificent, to remind people that all of this was his. He would tour the city today, now that the damage of the dragon attack was done. He would distribute coins here and there. Men remembered largess, and saw it as greatness, no matter what they had suffered before.

He looked out from his rooms to see that suffering, stepping close to the windows of the royal apartments so that he could survey the city that was his. The fires that had raged before were out by now, the damaged places lying empty against the skyline of the rest of Royalsport, like gaps in a fist fighter's smile. He briefly considered the things he would have his men build in place of the buildings there, with the buildings in the proper southern style, not the ugly square edges of the north.

He was still thinking about it when he saw the glint of steel in the distance. He stared at it, trying to make sense of it, and his years of war started to resolve that glint into armed men. More came, and more, lines of them marching and forming up. There were banners out there, flapping in the wind, too far to identify, and horses and foot soldiers.

Questions started to run through Ravin. Who were they? What was this force out there? Was there a chance that they could be friends come to aid him? No, obviously not. No one brought their army to swear fealty.

Not that it was much of an army. It was a mere puddle compared to the ocean of his own forces.

Yet it *was* there, out in front of *his* city, and such a thing would not stand.

Very carefully, he started to dress again, this time in his armor. He fit the pieces in place and hefted his sword, Heartsplitter. He had just finished when the hammering came on the door.

"Enter," Ravin said, and a single soldier came stumbling in, obviously pushed in by others, clearly not wanting to be there alone with his emperor's wrath. The man fell to his knees before Ravin, and the emperor considered him for a moment. "Speak."

"My emperor," the soldier said. "An army has come to the city, claiming to be led by... she calls herself Queen Lenore."

Ravin could see the man's terror as he said that, clearly convinced that Ravin would cut the head from his shoulders just for mentioning the princess's name. Ravin laughed as he walked back to the window, looking out at the force there.

It was almost pitifully small, and if it had some experienced men on the flanks, the center looked soft, ready to be destroyed.

"Tell me what she said," he commanded without looking around at the soldier.

"She said... she said that she wants you to face her forces on the ground before the city," the soldier said. "That she would take the city if she had to, but did not want to see it destroyed."

"And did you point out the weakness of her army?" Ravin asked.

"She said that her followers would fight harder because this... is their land, my emperor," the man said.

It sounded like the kind of thing the princess might believe: that because she was in the right, that would somehow translate into her soldiers being able to take on twice as many men as they otherwise would.

Ravin almost considered ignoring the threat completely; let them come and break against the walls of the city. Yet so soon after the dragon, he knew that he couldn't. It was better by far to assert his authority in this moment, to wipe out the pretender and display her broken body above the gates.

Yes, this could be a useful moment. His nobles could stand beside him on the field, seeing his strength. He would go out and destroy the enemy, their tactics came to naught. He would crush their pitiful attempts at siege weapons and use the wood to make pyres on which he had those he captured burned alive. Yes, this moment had all kinds of possibilities.

He turned to the soldier, who was still kneeling, awaiting his response.

"Go to the servants. Have them assemble my generals and my nobles. Open the castle gates and bring them in from the city. It is time to end this, once and for all."

By the time Ravin strode into the great hall of the castle, it was filled with northern nobles and with soldiers from all corners of the Southern Kingdom. In peace, they were fragmented, with men of the deserts at odds with those of the cities or the mountains. Moments like this brought them together, so that Ravin was almost grateful for the threat beyond the gate.

There were plenty of faces he recognized. Finnal was there with his father beside him, and a knot of nobles around them. Even his new sorcerer was there, although the young man looked more like some mercenary soldier than a great mystic. Ravin looked at each of them in turn, enjoying this moment, and the power he held in it.

"An army stands before the gates, led by a would-be usurper: Princess Lenore," he said.

That instantly got a murmur from the room, and Ravin found Finnal, the son of Duke Viris, speaking up.

"The rumor was that she had been slain," he pointed out.

"And today we make that rumor a reality," Ravin snapped back. "We will teach her that there is more to leading an army than sitting there waving a flag."

"And how will we do that, my emperor?" Finnal asked. He'd seemed more inclined to question in the last day or so, perhaps because his father had been shut out in the city. Still, it was a question Ravin welcomed, because it was a chance to set out what he required of all those there. He looked at the young man and his father, fixing them with his gaze. It was time for them to earn their newfound honors.

"The princess is trying to draw us out in one big strike against her center," Ravin said. "She has set out what look like siege engines, but I would guess that they are parts of fortifications. The idea is that we will charge at her and break against those fortifications, while her flanks close in to crush us."

Against a more foolish foe, it might have been an effective plan, but Ravin could see it for what it was. He had his counter stroke ready even now.

"We will appear to give them what they want," he said. He looked out over the mass of those there. The officers of his conquering army looked expectant, because they had seen him do this so many times before. They had heard him pick apart the plans of his foes and find ways to destroy them. The nobles didn't know enough of his skills to have that look yet, but they would; oh, they would.

"I will mass my troops by the main gates and march out to meet them in a head on fight," Ravin said. "I will appear to fall into their trap. Then, as they strike back, I will appear to give ground, drawing them in, closer to the city, narrowing their focus, making them throw all their efforts against that force."

He could see that moment now. If the princess had listened to so many stories that she believed she would win simply because she was in the right, then she would undoubtedly charge in after him, believing that one strike to the heart of his forces would finish things, bringing him down and scattering his men to the wind.

"While they close on the city," Ravin said, "my nobles will lead *their* forces, from the east and west gates. They will encircle the enemy out there."

He looked to Finnal, since the young man had been so quick to speak before.

"A most excellent plan, my emperor," he said, sweeping a bow.

Ravin snorted. "We'll see if you can *use* the fancy sword at your waist."

He turned from the young man before he could answer back, directing his attention to his new sorcerer.

"You..." he struggled for the name. He saw no reason to remember it until the boy proved himself.

"Anders, my emperor."

"Isn't this the time when your kind traditionally cast auguries?" he demanded.

The young man just stood there. "If you want me to, but I've always put sound tactics ahead of future seeing."

"So you won't offer me lightning from the sky to kill my foes?" Ravin asked. "Fire to consume them?"

He saw the boy shrug in response to that. "Do you need those things, my emperor? I have been spending my time considering the threat of dragons, but if you require me on the battlefield..."

There was a trap in that question, of course. Admit that he needed magic to win his victories, and Ravin would look weak, when today was about him looking strong. Even so, he wasn't happy that the sorcerer was avoiding the fight. Ravin would have to find a way to put him in his place before this was done.

"No, of course not," he snapped. "We will win without any of your tricks."

He turned from Anders to the rest of them, closing his hand tightly around the grip of his sword.

"I want to make one thing clear," he said. "As weak as this foe is, they still stand against my authority, and my rule. This ends today. Do not sweep in too early, in search of glory. Let them commit, let them be encircled, let them be destroyed."

He waited a moment longer, wanting that to sink in. Finally, it was time to make that clear.

"I don't want a single one of them to survive this day," he said. "Not one of them is to be permitted to escape, not one permitted to live to see the dawn. If any surrender, cut them down anyway. If any run, chase them and finish them."

By the time the sun set, the fields before the city would be red with the blood of his foes. They would run in his colors, and the Northern Kingdom would know, once and for all, who ruled it.

CHAPTER FOURTEEN

Vars groaned as he tried to rise. In truth, he still hurt too much to do it. He wanted nothing more than to stay asleep, but he knew that there was too much to do: bread to be baked, work to be done. If he didn't get up soon, Bethe would probably be there to scold him into wakefulness.

He smiled at the thought of actually wanting to get up to work. What kind of prince did that? Then again, he didn't look much like the prince he'd been right now. He was dressed in rough peasant clothing, his already dark hair made darker still by dirt. His features had once been fine, but now they were swollen from the beating he'd received at the hands of the soldiers who had come for Bethe.

He pushed himself up to his feet, the pain in his ribs and the bruises across his body making him wince with every movement.

"You don't need to get up," Bethe said from across the front room of her hut. She was already working on dough for the next batch of goods. A basket sat full of pastries, and to Vars's surprise, she brought one over to him, where normally she would have made him work hard first, on the basis that he wasn't likely to afterward.

"Thank you," Vars said.

"No, thank *you*," Bethe replied. "You got hurt saving my life, Vars. I think looking after you a little is the least that I can do."

Vars felt a hint of pride at her saying that, mixed in with shame. The pride was because he *had* saved Bethe; if he hadn't intervened, the soldiers would have carried her away to King Ravin, or just raped and killed her when she wouldn't go. He'd taken a beating to help her, had done what he'd wanted to do so badly and stepped in.

The shame came because he'd only done it accidentally. He'd been going to hide, going to hold back and hide in the wardrobe until it was all done. Only the fact that the guards had walked in before he could do it had propelled him into an animal kind of violence, aimed more at saving his own skin than anyone else's.

"You saved my life too," Vars pointed out. He'd never thought that a mere peasant would ever do anything like that for him, or that he would feel anything but contempt for them if they did. "You were the one who stabbed them both, after all."

He saw Bethe flinch as he said that, and he moved to her, putting a comforting arm around her. It wasn't something that would have come naturally to him at any other point, yet now, it seemed so obvious to do it, holding her close.

"No one will find the bodies now," Vars said. "Even if they do, they'll think it was the dragon attack."

The sight of the creature flying above the city had been terrifying, horrifying. The flames and the destruction had been enough to make it seem like the end of the world, but there had also been an opportunity in it. It had been hard to drag the bodies out of there, to throw them into a fallen, burning house, especially when Vars had been so hurt. Even so, they'd done it, and the bodies would be no more than crushed, burnt things by now.

"That's not... it was horrible, Vars," Bethe said. It only occurred to Vars then that she wasn't thinking about the practicalities of getting caught, but about the fear and the pain and the horror of what had been happening.

"I know," Vars said, "but it's done now. They're gone."

He surreptitiously reached out a hand to try to take a second pastry. Bethe slapped it away.

"Vars!" she said, but there was a faint smile there. Vars smiled too, even though once his response to a peasant doing something like that would have been to have her executed.

"What, can't your great savior eat now?" Vars asked.

"Not when *that* batch is meant to go to the people helping with the clean-up," Bethe said.

That was another thing that Vars would never understand about her. She barely made enough to live, and yet here she was about to give away things she could have been selling in order to make more. Yet Vars didn't complain; he knew that this was important to Bethe, even if he didn't really understand all of the reasoning behind it.

"Are you strong enough to help me carry this out to people?" Bethe asked.

Vars would rather have stayed inside, but it was probably better to pretend that things were normal. Enough people had seen him now that they might ask questions about why he wasn't there if he didn't help.

"What if they see my injuries?" he asked, trying to think of a good way to get out of it.

"We'll tell them that you got them pulling someone from a burning building," Bethe replied, and Vars couldn't tell if she was joking or not. Did she really see him as that heroic, or was the point that she saw through him better than anyone, to the coward beneath?

He certainly saw her in a different light now. When he'd first met her, Vars had found himself angry that a peasant would dare to tell him what to do, kept there only by the fact that he had nowhere else to go. Oh, she'd been attractive enough, but he'd had the great beauties of the court to choose from, so why should that matter?

Now *she* mattered to him. It wasn't just that she seemed more beautiful by the day to Vars; he actually found himself caring about her. He wanted her to be safe, and he wanted to be the kind of man that she believed him to be, even though that man was a long way from anything Vars actually was.

He moved closer to her. This close, and she was almost achingly beautiful in spite of the bruises the guards had inflicted on her as well. He wanted nothing more in that moment than to close the distance between them, and just for a heartbeat or two, it seemed as if Bethe might want the same thing. Vars could feel the tension there between them, and there was something about it that terrified him and excited him in ways that being this close to other women hadn't. Maybe it was because with them, he hadn't cared.

Bethe seemed to be feeling a lot of the same things. She had a look in her eye that Vars couldn't place, but that seemed to promise so much.

So slowly that it hurt, and not just because of the bruising, they started to close the distance between them.

The sound of heavy boots moving in step cut through the moment, making Vars jerk back, his head snapping round.

"Vars, what is it?" Bethe asked. "Did I misunderstand? Did I do something wrong?"

"Soldiers," Vars said, because while booted feet were common enough among the men who went out to work in the city's tougher jobs, that level of coordination wasn't. Vars knew marching when he heard it. "Listen."

Bethe listened for a moment or two, and Vars saw her face pale in obvious fear. It matched his own.

"They've found out about the others," Bethe said. "Or they've come looking now that their friends haven't come back. What are we going to do? We need to run."

Vars caught her arm as she headed for the door, not because he was any braver than she was, but because he'd had far more experience of being a coward.

"You don't run blindly from things," Vars said. That was how he'd ended up here, after all. "You work out what the danger is, and that way, you know what you need to avoid. What if we run out there and they're waiting for us? What if we run, and it turns out we could have bluffed our way out of this?"

He was no kind of hero, but this situation didn't call for one. It needed a well-practiced coward, and there was none better at avoiding danger than Vars. Vars had spent his life dodging trouble, avoiding the consequences of the things he'd done. He knew better than anyone when to try to talk his way out of things, when to lie, when to run.

He could think of a hundred different ways that this could play out, and strangely, he found himself rejecting out of hand the ones where he shoved Bethe into danger in order to buy himself time to escape. It made no sense, but his entire being seemed fixed on that. He needed to find another way.

Keeping low, Vars scurried to the windows of the house, peeking through its shutters, trying to get a sense of the danger approaching. Was it a couple of guards or a full squad? Were they going to encircle the house or just approach from the front? Vars's mind was racing with the possibilities, and what each would mean for escape.

What he saw as he looked through carefully, trying to keep out of sight, made him freeze. Rank after rank of soldiers marched past, a whole army's worth of them making their way through the city toward the gates. Horns blared to command them, and drums beat to ensure that they marched in step. Horses trotted alongside them, the riders checking short bows and lances.

For the briefest, most wonderful moment, Vars felt relief. A force this size had nothing to do with him or Bethe; it was merely passing by. These weren't soldiers come to execute them for what they'd done, but ones off about some business he couldn't begin to fathom.

Vars jerked back, breathing hard, as he saw Emperor Ravin riding among them, golden armored and riding a horse larger than any of the others.

"What is it?" Bethe asked. "What's happening?"

A different kind of fear came to Vars then, of the unknown, but also of the dangers that might be coming.

"I'm not sure," he said. "I think ... I think there's going to be a battle."

CHAPTER FIFTEEN

F innal stood with his father, Duke Viris, outside the gates of the castle, gathering nobles and their retinues. Side by side, and the similarities between the two were obvious, both tall, slender, commanding. They were both dressed in the black and silver of their house, although now both wore armor plate over their noble dress. Finnal rested his hand on his sword, knowing that appearing as a warrior would be more important than *being* one this day.

Around him, others shouted orders as they arranged their retinues, striving for attention and authority within the mass of the remaining nobles. Finnal and his father did not, for two reasons. First, Finnal knew that their orders would ultimately be the ones obeyed here; their retinue obeyed absolutely, and the other nobles knew their places in the hierarchy of things.

Second, it was better to speak in quiet voices when considering the downfall of an emperor.

"Things have gone far enough, Father," Finnal said softly, leaning against a horse rail as an excuse to keep apart from the rest of those there.

"What our agent said is certainly proving true," his father agreed.

Finnal thought of Aurelle, so beautiful if one liked that kind of thing, and so useful in getting rid of Prince Greave. She had been the one to point out that ultimately, they would never be more than servants to a man like the emperor. At the time, the words had brought no more than a faint doubt at the back of Finnal's mind, but now, he could see that it was the truth.

"He shut you out of the castle, leaving you for the dragon," Finnal said. "He speaks to me like I'm nothing, let alone the son of a duke."

Ordinarily, he would have picked his words more carefully, but now the clatter of weapons being taken up and men moving into position covered it a little. Besides, anyone listening was likely to be his man, or his father's.

"True," Duke Viris said. "At the same time, I am not inclined to throw my life away as Queen Aethe did. With a man like Ravin, you act or you do not. You are his wholehearted friend, or you see him dead, nothing in between."

"The battle presents an opportunity," Finnal suggested.

His father seemed more thoughtful. "Perhaps. It will depend how things play out."

Finnal respected his father's abilities when it came to planning, but here it seemed that this was as good a chance as they would get.

"My wife is facing our emperor in a battle where anything could happen," he pointed out. "When is a better chance at power likely to come?"

"Perhaps never," his father agreed. "But it is also a chance to throw our lives away if we play this wrong, my son. Opportunities are plentiful; it is about how one exploits them."

Finnal knew the look in his father's eye well enough by now to understand what it meant. "You have a plan."

Duke Viris nodded. "We start by waiting to see how the battle is going. If Ravin overwhelms Lenore's forces easily, then we pile in at the last moment so that we seem his loyal servants. We lose nothing. If things are closer fought, though, then it would be an easy thing to seem to come to the aid of the victor and perhaps..."

"Perhaps battles are chaotic places where someone might fall to an unseen blade?" Finnal suggested. "Leaving either their husband or their most loyal noble to step into the breach?"

His father smiled. "Exactly."

Finnal liked the plan. It was simple, and elegant, and safe. All they had to do was wait, and tell the other nobles that they were waiting for the perfect moment to strike. He stood there, contemplating all the ways that he might benefit from today, and that was when he saw one person he hadn't been expecting to see: the boy from the House of Weapons, the one who had presented him with the sword he wore upon his wedding day.

When Devin had seen the armies massing, he'd known that the moment had come to make his way to the castle. He didn't know whose army this was, or why it was there, but it seemed like the best chance he had to get into the castle. The last of the fires in the city was out, and he'd regained the strength he needed. There would never be a better opportunity to slip inside than during the chaotic gathering of Ravin's forces.

The only downside was that Sigil couldn't approach closer than the shadows of one of the nearby buildings. There were too many men who might spot the wolf now, and the plan was to slip in unnoticed. For the first part of it, the plan seemed to work perfectly; with so many men gathering in the space beyond the castle, it was easy for Devin to step in among them.

Then he'd spotted Finnal and his father, and it had just seemed so obvious to creep closer to them. Perhaps it was because their very presence there told Devin just how deeply they'd betrayed Lenore, and in that moment a part of him wanted to put a knife in both of them for that. Perhaps it was because he half hoped that he might be able to use them to get deeper into the castle. Either way, he slipped forward silently.

When he got closer, what he heard only made the sick anger inside him grow. Not content with just siding with Ravin, they were now planning on betraying whoever the winner of the battle was? If they'd been alone, Devin would have cut them down there and then. Even as it was, he felt for his connection to the magic, thinking of all the ways he might use it to attack.

Only the thought of what he was there to do held Devin back. There were other dangers in this kingdom besides these men. He needed to get to the spot where Anders would be going, needed to take back what Anders had stolen.

He saw one thing that might help with that sitting on Finnal's hip. The first sword he'd made from star metal shone there, and Devin wanted to run up and snatch it from him, cutting down the man who'd never been worthy to wear it, or to marry Lenore. He knew he had to find another way, though. The only question was how.

One possibility occurred to Devin as he listened to them talking about betrayal: he could simply walk up and demand the sword as his price for remaining silent. Devin didn't like that idea though, and not just because the thought of blackmailing even someone like this felt wrong. He suspected that it wouldn't work. Men as powerful as this didn't respond to blackmail with anything but violence. They would probably plunge the sword through his heart rather than give it to him.

What did that leave, then? This wasn't a situation for violence or magic, cruel leverage or even asking openly, unless ...

Devin smiled as a solution came to him. Stepping from the shadows, he approached Finnal and his father, stopping short of them and sweeping the best bow that he could muster.

"I know you, boy, don't I?" Finnal said. "You were ... you were the one to give me this sword."

"Devin of the House of Weapons, my lord," Devin said. "I am honored that you remember me."

It made bile rise in Devin's throat to speak so flatteringly to a man like this. Still, Finnal seemed to take it as no more than his due, and Devin knew that he had made the right choice.

"What are you doing here?" he demanded. "Do you have a place here? I know Prince Rodry saw amusement in keeping you around, but do you think it's normal for a peasant to approach his betters like this?"

"Forgive me, my lord," Devin said, using another bow to disguise his hatred of the other young man. "Emperor Ravin decided that my skills as a smith were of use to his forces."

He knew that was a lie that would be hard to question. A man like the emperor would always need more weapons.

"What are you doing here, boy?" Duke Viris demanded, and his tone was colder and more calculating than his son's.

Now for the harder lie.

"The emperor heard that I could work with star metal," Devin said, "and he questioned me about it. I ... I told him about the blade I had made for your wedding to ... to Princess Lenore."

He saw Finnal's hand close over the hilt of it reflexively.

"I'm sorry, my lords, I could not lie to him," Devin said. With other men, he suspected that this fearful peasant act would be too much. In truth though, this was what men like Finnal and Duke Viris saw when they spoke to others. It was what they *expected.*

"Nor should you," Duke Viris said. "He is our emperor, after all."

"He wants my sword?" Finnal said.

Devin nodded. "That's what he said, my lord, when he sent me for it. He said that it would be fitting for an emperor to wield a sword made... made at the command of King Godwin."

It seemed strange thinking back to that moment, back when Lenore... when she'd been *alive*. It hurt to think of it, but Devin knew that he needed to do this.

"I'm sorry, my lords," Devin said. "I would not have come, but he commanded me."

He saw Finnal and his father looking to one another, and he could guess what they were thinking: even though they didn't want to give up such a fine weapon, they wanted to appear disloyal even less. The sword was just a sword to them, after all, while seeming loyal would give them more chance of betraying Ravin successfully when the moment came.

Duke Viris broke the silence. "You do not need to apologise, boy, for following the commands of your ruler. I hope that you will always be so obedient. Finnal, give this boy your sword."

"Yes, Father," Finnal said, although he hid his annoyance less well. He slid the scabbard from his belt, passing it to Devin. "Tell the emperor that we remain his loyal subjects, and look forward to seeing his enemies' blood on this blade."

"I will, my lord," Devin said as he took the sword.

He hurried away, trying not to show any of the satisfaction he felt as he did it. It wasn't just that he'd managed to get this sword out of the hands of a man who had never deserved it; it was that he now had a weapon that might just be able to stand against Anders.

CHAPTER SIXTEEN

As he crept back in the direction of Royalsport, Renard couldn't help asking himself exactly what he was doing. Logic dictated that he should be going in the other direction, away from the potential fighting, away from the amulet and the other threats that it could bring. Yet here he was, sneaking his way through the outer slums of it, moving back toward the walled interior.

All because Queen Lenore had commanded it. Renard frowned at that. Why was *he,* of all people, taking the orders of a queen? She hadn't even offered him coin for doing it, or a pardon, or any of the other things that a ruler would typically offer someone like him.

Maybe that was a part of it, that she'd treated him like a human being rather than just something to be used and discarded. Maybe another part of it was that the amulet was still waiting beneath a pile of rubble, and succeeding in this would create the best opportunity to get it safely within the apparatus the sorcerer had said would contain it.

To his surprise, though, more of it was that he genuinely wanted Lenore to succeed. He'd seen what cruel rulers could do, how hard life could be under men like Lord Carrick, and now Ravin. Renard had no wish to live under rulers like that; it was hard enough dodging guards who were bound by rules, without having to avoid ones who could grab you at random, as well.

The final part was … well, it fit with what Meredith wanted, and *that* couldn't be underestimated. So Renard would get into the city, go back to the House of Sighs, and do everything he'd been asked to do.

First, though, he needed to get in. Reaching the outer city under cover of darkness had been easy enough, but the rest might be more difficult with an army sitting on the open ground beyond. This wasn't a situation where a quick disguise and a well-crafted story would let him saunter in, as he had with Aurelle.

The main gate was out, of course. The guards on it would be alert now, and there could very well be an army coming the other way any minute. The same probably went for any of the major gates of the city.

That left the minor ones, the sealed up places, all the old smugglers' routes. Before, it had been unthinkable that he could have used any of them, because of course a man as cunning as Ravin would have them watched, and sealed, and more. Now though, if he was gathering his army to strike at Lenore's, those men would probably be pulled back into the whole, away from guarding spots that they didn't see as relevant.

It wasn't much of a hope, but it still gave Renard a chance. And if there *were* guards, he had two long knives strapped to the small of his back. He might not be Erin, willing to plunge into the fray at a moment's notice, but he could still fight when he needed to.

Renard crept along the wall, moving from house to house, low wall to fence. There might not be guards on the smaller gates, but there *would* be men on the walls, all too ready to send down an arrow. Renard paused in the shadow of a building, considering his next steps.

When the moment seemed right, he sprinted forward, heading for the next piece of cover, and the next. All his old instincts kicked in, so that he could pick out all the ways that each object could hide someone. He saw the way a washing line offered false hope, since the washing on it would billow and shift too much. He saw the way the seemingly slender posts of a carpenter's workshop could hide him at just the right angle.

Renard kept moving forward, and ahead, he saw what he was looking for: an old, low gate that was more for dumping rubble and rubbish beyond the wall than really for people to go through. It was sealed up now with locks and with spars of wood set at angles, making it impossible to get through.

Renard set about removing those spars one by one. Since he wasn't weakened by the amulet now, he had some of his old strength. Even so, each one was an effort, making him sweat and strain just to move the wood enough that he could slip through.

Then there were the locks, three in total, because it was clear that when this gate had been sealed, no one was meant to get through. Renard considered the locks in turn, one big and clunky, one smaller and more elegant, the last older and almost rusted through. It was like each succeeding generation had been more emphatic than the last that no one would get in this way except when needed. Frankly, Renard was amazed that they hadn't bricked it up.

He set to work on the locks, one at a time. The first thing he did was to take a small vial of penetrating oil and pour the contents into the rusted lock. It would take time to work, and Renard wanted this to take as little time as possible. He started work on the newest looking of the locks first, reasoning that it would be the most sophisticated and hardest to pick.

It felt good to have lockpicks in his hands again, rather than running hither and yon, trying to avoid dragons. There was an art to this, and a feel that never truly left the fingers. Renard could feel the tumblers of the lock now, working out where each one wanted to be as gently as if he were teasing a thorn from a wild animal's paw or brushing a stray strand of hair from a lover's face.

Why did he think of Meredith when he thought of that?

One answer was the kiss she'd given him before he'd left. It had been a good kiss, of course, because they'd both had their share of practice over the years, especially given her profession. It had felt like more than that, though, something beautiful, something meaningful...

Renard was so caught up in his memories that he almost didn't notice the trap. The wire was slender, almost invisible, and definitely new. Renard's picks were already resting against it when he noticed it, the pressure of them just gently distending it, without quite pulling it hard enough to set off whatever lay there. Renard pulled back, ever so carefully, breathing hard.

As gently as he could, he traced the wire to where it wrapped around a simple glass globe, no bigger than Renard's fist, filled with something billowing and green. Apparently, Ravin's Quiet Men had found a simpler way to protect this gate than putting guards on it. Renard wasn't certain what the substance was, but he *was* sure that he wouldn't want to inhale any of it. Moving slowly, he cut the wire, then took the orb and flung it from him, into an open space.

Glass shattered, and green smoke rose. Briefly, it flared, the air itself enough to ignite whatever alchemical substance lay within it. Renard didn't want to think about what it would have done to his lungs if he'd breathed any of it in.

He returned his attention to the complexity of the first lock, and now he had the feel of it, he could move its elements into alignment with the precision of some scholar's orrery. Renard heard it click, and set to work on the next lock. No sooner had he done it, than he saw something moving out of the corner of his eye. A guard was approaching along the top of the wall.

For a second, Renard froze in place. He was partially hidden by the wall where he was, but how much longer would that last? Would he be safest retreating to another piece of cover?

No, that didn't work: the guard would spot him in the open ground. Worse, if Renard stayed where he was, the man would probably see him as soon as he got overhead. That meant that his only real hope was to get through the locks and out to the other side of the wall before the guard reached him.

Renard threw himself back into working on the second lock. He'd expected it to be simpler because it was older, but if anything there were more moving parts to it. He could feel himself sweating as he worked on them, trying to line up each piece in turn. It seemed like forever before he head the lock click, and as he glanced up, he could see that the guard was still heading toward him.

Renard set to work on the last lock, and it wouldn't budge. The components of it felt as though they had some movement to them, but they resisted his attempts to move them. He could maybe force them, but the danger in that was that his tools might snap off in the lock, leaving him no choice but to break the door open or find another way. Neither would work with a guard so close.

Ideally, he would have applied more oil, waited longer, then set about it in silence. With the soldier getting closer by the moment, though, there was no time for it. Renard forced the tumblers of the lock to move, feeling their pressure against his tools, hearing them creak as he worked on them.

He could feel his tools bending, feel his fingers pushing them to their limits. Any more pressure, and the thin metal of the tools would break, any more force, and he would be stuck looking at the stubs of them.

Renard's heart almost jumped out of his chest as he heard a click, and he stared down at his tools, but no, they were whole. The lock was open.

With a sigh of relief, he threw himself through the gates, heading for the House of Sighs and the job he still had to do.

CHAPTER SEVENTEEN

Nerra clung to Shadr's back as the two of them swooped toward their next target. Up here, she could feel the pure joy of the flight, the exhilaration that came from the freedom to cover the kingdom with ease.

There will be more joy when the human-things burn, Shadr sent to her.

Nerra wasn't so sure about that. She understood the necessity, given the cruelty of the humans, but she wasn't sure that she could take joy in it.

"I was thinking that we should leave more alive," she said.

They will not fear us if we do not kill them, Shadr insisted.

"They'll fear you," Nerra assured her. Shadr was more powerful than any of them could hope to be, more powerful even than other dragons. Her command of fire and shadow meant that she could swoop from the open sky without being seen until she wanted, that she could burn and freeze, hurt and terrify with the magic that lay behind her breath. Who could fail to fear her?

You must not fear me, my princess. It is together that we will rule everything.

No, Nerra didn't fear her. Shadr had chosen her in a way that she hadn't known it was possible to be chosen. She had helped her to become more than she had ever been before. Nerra knew her on a deeper level than anyone else; even her sisters couldn't see into the heart of her being as Shadr could. Nerra didn't fear the dragon, but the sheer enormity of what they were doing made nerves rise in her.

Below, she could see the green of the countryside, farms dotted here and there. Those weren't the targets now, though. Burning farms could create some terror, but other things were likely to make people talk faster.

The dark ribbon of a road stretched out across the landscape, and there were dots moving along that ribbon, close enough to one another that they could have been a line of ants. Nerra knew that they were wagons, and as she and Shadr got closer, her enhanced eyesight started to pick out people and horses, oxen and wooden-sided carts.

These were not the simple carts of farmers, for the most part. Instead, they were merchant carts, there to move large numbers of goods across the kingdom. With the currents of the Slate, it was often easier to do it that way rather than trying to move everything on the treacherous sea.

Nerra could see soldiers around some of the carts, serving as guards. They were dressed in King Ravin's colors, obviously providing protection to the convoys for a price, or maybe just asserting his control over trade within the kingdom. The convoys on this road were like blood rushing along an artery, providing a much-needed flow of goods between the Northern Kingdom's towns.

These would not reach those who needed them.

"I don't want us to hurt the merchants," Nerra said to Shadr.

They are all human-things, Shadr replied.

"Soldiers are one thing," Nerra said. "But the merchants are just people going about their lives."

She found herself thinking of those who had died on the farm. It saddened her that so many had needed to die. Only the need to stop what the amulet could do made it necessary. She would not allow the slaughter of dragons and their kin again, even if it meant destroying the human-things who were trying to kill them.

Why should we spare them? Shadr asked.

"More people left alive means more people to tell others what is happening," Nerra pointed out.

Shadr gave a rumble that might have been a sound of annoyance. Certainly, Nerra could feel her frustration through the link between them.

Very well.

She dove, fast and straight as an arrow, so that the wind whipped around Nerra, and she had to dig the claws of her hands into Shadr's scales in order to keep from being thrown from the dragon's back. She heard Shadr roar, the sound booming out over the line of the road, and now the tiny figures below stood, and pointed, and eventually screamed.

They ran from their carts, scattering toward the sides of the road as Shadr swooped in toward the carts. The dragon queen opened her mouth wide enough that it could have swallowed someone whole, and flames poured from her in a line that set carts aflame like a string of candles.

Nerra felt the heat, saw the carts catch fire one after another. A cart of rich clothes burned higher than most, a stock of perfumes burst with the scent of flowers coming even over the scorched scent of burning wood and flesh. Horses and oxen screamed as the fires consumed them, and Nerra winced.

Shadr landed on her hind legs, the dragon towering over the people, the carts, the animals. She snatched up one of the flame-scorched oxen in her foreclaws, and her great jaws clamped down on it, biting it in half with ease. Nerra could feel enough of the dragon to know that the picture the move presented was intentional, with blood spilling over her scales in an image out of nightmares.

Dismount, Shadr commanded her, and Nerra slid down from Shadr's back. Even as she did it, some of the soldiers there seemed to remember that they were supposed to protect the convoy, even from horrors such as this. Drawing swords, they ran forward to the spot where Shadr stood.

The dragon plunged toward them in turn, her mouth opening to burn one with a gout of flame, her claws sweeping out to rip another man apart. A third came at the dragon queen from the side, and her tail swept round to send him flying.

Nerra stood there, watching the carnage as it unfolded. A soldier struck at Shadr, but the thick scales of her hide turned the blow aside, and the dragon's head whipped around to clamp huge jaws down on him. Another tried to stab at her neck, and Shadr's claws plunged through him, pinning him to the ground.

One of the men had the sense to run past Shadr, swinging at Nerra instead. Nerra had the speed to avoid the blow now, and she shoved the man back from her. She saw Shadr turn, obviously sensing that Nerra was in danger through the connection between them, and she loomed above the soldier then.

"No," Nerra breathed, but the dragon did not listen. Instead, Shadr breathed the shadows of her name, mixed with fire, deadly enough to strip the man's flesh from his bones as he screamed.

You are mine! No one threatens you!

The other soldiers were running by now, and Shadr sent a blast of flame after them, catching one and bringing him down. The others got clear, though, throwing themselves into the fields beyond the road, trying to find somewhere to hide.

"The wagons," Nerra insisted. "We need to finish destroying the wagons."

Shadr roared at being held back from killing like that, but she did it anyway, flames rushing out to consume the few wagons that had not been set ablaze in Shadr's initial swooping strike.

To one side, Nerra could see a cluster of merchants and porters cowering, obviously trying to decide if they could escape by running or not. Nerra could feel Shadr's readiness for more violence, and she knew that if the human-things ran then, the dragon would descend on them without mercy.

Nerra stepped forward to them before they could do anything so stupid. She raised her voice as she gestured to Shadr.

"You still live by the grace of the dragon queen, Shadr," she said. "You live so that you might tell others what you have seen here today. I am her chosen, Princess Nerra of the Northern Kingdom."

She looked around at the men, taking in their fear, their horror at the strangeness and the violence of everything they were seeing.

"Today, you have lost your goods and your animals," Nerra said. "But you will keep your lives, because you have not sought to stand against the dragon queen. All those who do shall die. Those human-things who reject the rule of the dragon queen will die." She took a step toward them. "Go. Go tell others what you have seen here. Tell them all."

Now they ran, and because they were doing it at Nerra's command, Shadr let them. Instead, the dragon feasted on another flame-seared animal. When she was done, she lowered her neck to let Nerra climb atop her once more.

"How many more?" Nerra asked.

Until the human-things send out their champion with the amulet, Shadr replied. *Until they come to face me.*

That was the point of all this, after all. There was a reason that they were burning a clear line across the country, so that anyone tracing their trail of terror would be able to track them, or even try to get ahead and wait for them.

Still, it was a lot of death and destruction.

It is what is needed, Shadr sent. *We need to draw out their champion, force them to fight, and kill them. We need to take the amulet from them.*

"How do we do that, when the amulet has such power?" Nerra asked. She doubted that even Shadr could stand against the power of the amulet directly.

I cannot, Shadr admitted. *At least, not with certainty. That is why we will pick the place where we fight. We will wait for them where we can see them coming as they approach. Then, as they try to come to face me, you will be the one to kill them.*

"Me?" Nerra said. She hadn't thought to the end of this, hadn't considered that she would be the one who would have to finish this when Shadr couldn't.

You are my chosen, Nerra. We are linked so that you can do the things that I cannot, sworn to protect and defend me, to obey.

"I know," Nerra said.

You will slay the one who comes, Shadr instructed her. *You have the strength, and the skill. You will kill them, and open the way for us to take back this world.*

Nerra knew how much that meant. She said the only thing she could as Shadr spread her wings to take to the air again.

"It will be an honor, my queen."

CHAPTER EIGHTEEN

In theory, Odd should have been good at waiting. All his hours at the monastery should have taught him that much at least. Instead, he found thoughts racing through his head as he sat beside Lenore at the heart of her army: thoughts of everything that might happen today, thoughts of the death to follow.

It would almost be easier once the enemy made their attack. Then there would be the flow of battle around him, the complete immersion in the one thing that Odd truly knew how to do. He laughed at the thought that only *he* could think of the middle of a battle as more peaceful than sitting on a horse, then looked round to find the others staring at him.

It wasn't just Lenore, Erin, and Greave. Odd could see the nervousness of the peasant folk there too. They probably didn't like having such a famed madman for their commander. Odd smiled over at one of them.

"Lovely day for a battle, at least," he said. "The worst ones are when it's raining. All the horses get bogged down, and the mud means you can't see who you're killing."

The man gave him a rictus smile of nerves. Odd couldn't claim to be a great orator like Lenore.

"Tell me, are you afraid?" Odd asked. "Afraid to be standing so near to Oderick the Mad?"

Yet there *was* a point to all this. Let the men see that he wasn't afraid, play up to what they thought of him, and they remembered just who they had on their side.

"Um ... yes?" the man said.

"Well," Odd said, pointing at the gates. "Imagine what *they're* feeling. You're all standing beside me. For all they know, you're all like me."

That got them thoughtful, at least.

"And you know what, lads? You *are*. You have that same thing deep down inside you, that same fire. I know, I can see these things. When the time comes, you'll be afraid, but that will only fuel that fire. You'll charge forward, and you'll make them fear *you*."

"That was well done," Lenore whispered to him.

"I can't inspire men half as well as you, my queen," Odd said. He saw the gates of the city start to open. "It's time."

He saw Lenore turn to Erin and Greave. "Go now, both of you."

Erin had argued before, but she didn't now, obviously sensing that a moment this close to a battle was not the moment to question her sister's commands. She might not look happy, but she wheeled her horse along with Greave, heading back over the farmland behind them, toward the line of the trees.

Meanwhile, Odd returned his attention to the city gates. Men were starting to pour from them now, flooding out into the slums beyond, marching through them and starting to form up before the city.

Some commanders might have sounded the charge in that moment, hoping to catch the enemy while they were still forming up, but Odd knew the dangers. Charge now, and they *might* take an unwary enemy by surprise, but it was more likely that they would give up their own carefully picked ground only to stumble into whatever trap Ravin was setting for them.

In any case, that wasn't the plan.

They marched from the city, little by little, forming up in their battle line. Odd noted that they'd gone for something dangerous: an oblique line with the heaviest troops all clustered on one flank. No doubt the idea was to slam into the strong side of Lenore's lines with enough weight to overcome it, then roll up the rest from there.

"Should we reposition?" Lenore asked him, obviously seeing the danger.

Odd shook his head. "This close to them, it would invite their charge while we did it. They would strike us before we were set, and it would be worse."

Lenore nodded. "Then we stick to the plan."

That was one of the good points about her: she might not have been raised to be a battle commander, but she understood her own weaknesses, and she knew how to make clear, good decisions with the right information. Odd just hoped that he was *giving* her the right information.

For almost the first time ever before a battle, Odd found himself feeling nervous. It wasn't the killing or the potential for dying that had him feeling that way, though, it was all the people looking to him, relying on him, to keep them alive. If he gave Lenore the wrong advice, she might pay with her life, and the lives of all the others who had come to aid her.

"There are so many of them," Lenore said.

He looked out at the enemy's forces. There were a lot of them, certainly more than their force. They spread out like a bloody wound across the landscape, the red and purple of their uniforms like dripping blood. Yet the army wasn't as large as it could have been. This wasn't every soldier Ravin had brought northward with him, because plenty of *those* had been sent on to take other places, to guard caravans, to impose his new order over the kingdom. This was not a vast sea of enemies that would swallow them up without a trace.

"We'll hold," Odd said. "We have to."

Odd tried to pick out the various pieces of their foes. There were desert horse archers in a wedge, weapons ready for use. No doubt they would try for harrying attacks, skimming past the flanks of their force as they let shafts fly. More conventional missile troops stood in ranks further back, crossbow men mostly, but some with long bows and hunting bows. Odd suspected that their own peasant archers might actually be able to keep up a better rate of fire, even though there were fewer of them.

Solid-looking infantry in scale and banded armor formed the majority of the forces there, with some light troops in chain carrying short swords and hatchets, skirmishers from the cities of the south. There were wild-looking axe men in a group, and a unit in plate armor who could have been knights, carrying longswords and with round shields strapped to their arms.

"It's tricky, holding so many disparate elements together," Odd said. "If we're lucky, holes will appear in their lines as they move."

"How likely is it?" Lenore asked.

Odd didn't know. In truth, the southern forces had already shown that they could work together well, with Ravin's force of will holding them together in spite of whatever differences they had.

"Not very," Odd said. "But we can hope."

Staring out there, he could make out the man himself, resplendent in gilded armor, his two-handed sword held with an easy lightness that belied its size. He sat atop a black stallion larger than any of the other horses there, protected by gilded barding that mirrored its owner's armor.

He sat there atop his horse while his army continued to form up around him, and now Odd was starting to suspect that it was doing so with deliberate slowness, in order to give the fear in Lenore's forces more time in which to build, and to allow their excitement to give way to tiredness.

It was a small thing, but it was also a reminder of just how thoroughly Ravin knew the business of war. This was a man who had fought throughout his life, who had commanded men in battles large and small. He had fought to unify his kingdom, and then to take this one.

More than that, he'd shown how cunning he was in all the arts of a ruler. He had survived assassination attempts and outthought potential rivals. He had probably had as many men murdered as he'd faced in open combat, and at the same time had managed to make allies of men who would otherwise have been his enemies.

It all amounted to a man they could not afford to underestimate.

Lenore was obviously thinking the same thing, because she looked over to Odd and gestured back to the would-be emperor.

"What will his plan be?" Lenore asked.

"It's hard to be sure," Odd replied. "He might be direct about it, as a double bluff."

"You don't think he will, though," Lenore said.

Odd shook his head. "Every time people have faced him, he's had *some* plan. He manipulated your father into battle by kidnapping you. He found a safe way to invade by taking Leveros. He ambushed the Knights of the Spur. He found a way into the city. He used a double to survive your mother's uprising. He won't fight a battle like this without having a trick set up. Wherever he seems to want us to look, we should watch out for a dagger coming toward our backs."

With a man like Ravin, it was almost inevitable. More than that, it was something they were almost relying on.

Odd was still thinking about that when Ravin dismounted his horse and came forward from his lines, walking with the slow confidence of a man who didn't have anything to fear. He set his sword in the dirt, point first, and Odd found himself reminded far too much of the way Lenore had demanded a parley with her banner.

"He wants to talk," Lenore said.

"What is there left to talk *about*?" Odd asked.

Lenore considered that. "If we can find a way to end this peacefully, many people will not die today. I have to at least try talking to him."

She started to dismount.

"Have you considered the possibility that this is his trick?" Odd asked her. "It could be that he's formed up his army, when his real plan is simply to cut you down as soon as you're close enough."

"I know," Lenore said. "But I *have* to do this. I will not ask my men to charge forward if I am too afraid to try to negotiate."

She set off in the direction of the waiting emperor, alone.

Chapter Nineteen

L enore could feel her heart in her mouth as she walked toward the waiting emperor. A part of her felt certain that this was going to be a trap, that Ravin was going to cut her down the moment she reached him. It might have been more comforting to bring Odd with her, rather than leaving him with her lines, but even if she had Ravin might be able to strike so quickly that he couldn't do anything to stop it.

She knew the dangers, but still she walked forward, toward the spot where Ravin waited with his sword stuck in the dirt, his gauntleted hands resting on the pommel. Lenore came forward to a distance where they could have shouted to one another, then to one where they could have talked simply by raising their voices. At each potential stopping point, the mockery of Ravin's gaze made her take the next few steps.

"I was not sure you would come alone," Ravin said. "I thought a girl like you would be afraid that I would cut you down."

"*My* army can survive without me," Lenore said. "Kill me, and my men will cut you down in turn. I am not a so-called emperor whose empire will fall apart without him."

She heard Ravin let out a grim laugh as she stepped forward to meet him. She thought she saw his hand tense on the pommel of his sword, and felt a thrill of fear run through her. He started forward just slightly, and Lenore had to keep herself from reacting. This was him testing her, trying to work out how she would react.

"You think that you know me," he said as she got close enough to talk. "You think you see what I am. You say that my empire would fall apart without me, as if that is an *insult*."

"If you stood for something bigger than yourself, you'd understand," Lenore replied.

"And what do you stand for, girl?" Ravin asked. "Some vague ideal of niceness and gentleness? It is not how the world works. Some parochial idea of throwing out all those who do not belong in *your* kingdom? You stand for nothing except your own place in the world."

Lenore shook her head. "You could never understand."

"I understand that I brought my kingdom together," Ravin said. "I stopped all the petty wars. I brought together factions that had been killing one another for generations. I made our kingdom *great* and gave it *direction.*"

"By pointing it at others for invasion," Lenore said.

"By rejoining what should always have been one kingdom," Ravin replied. Lenore saw him move again, and still, she forced herself not to react. "You are braver than I thought you would be. You have achieved a lot, but this is where it ends for you."

"Unless we end *you,*" Lenore shot back.

"You won't," Ravin said. "Your people will fight bravely, of course, because you will tell them that they have right on their side. They will throw themselves forward with enthusiasm, sure that they must win. And they will die."

He made it sound like a certainty, and Lenore had to remind herself that it wasn't, that it was just him trying to unsettle her.

Ravin kept going. "If you fight, I have given my men instructions to take no prisoners, to kill every single man and woman they find on the battlefield. As I did with your mother's pitiful rebellion."

Lenore had to swallow back her anger at that. It was hard, so very hard.

"You're trying to provoke me," Lenore said.

Ravin smiled. "Maybe not so foolish. As you say, I hold together many factions. Some of those believe in the importance of honor at times like this."

"So you can't just strike me down," Lenore guessed.

"Oh, I *could,*" Ravin assured her. "You couldn't stop me. Shall I tell you how easily I beat your sister when I fought her?"

"You can't," Lenore said, "or you'd have done it by now. You want me to make the first move to give you an excuse."

She thought about what would happen then. Her forces would be angry, and would charge to try to avenge her. They would abandon their carefully crafted plan, and Ravin's forces would destroy them.

"Say what your brought me here to say," Lenore said.

Ravin shrugged. "You claim to care about your people; prove it. Surrender to me, here and now. Kneel and declare fealty."

"And then you'll...what, have me killed by Quiet Men? Tie me to a stake and kill me?" Lenore demanded.

"Worse," Ravin said. "I'll have a priest brought out here, and I'll marry you."

Lenore stared at him in shock.

"Such things often end wars," Ravin said. "Your pitiful army will see that things are done, and will be permitted to melt back into obscurity. Your family will have no reason to fight. The alternative is that you bring about hundreds, even thousands, of deaths. You have one chance."

Lenore could hardly believe, after all this, that he had made the offer. But then, she could feel what his plan was: to get her angry, to stop her thinking. It had been what he'd done to her brother Rodry. Now, she needed to keep her cool. She stood there, trying to choose her next words with care. Then she smiled, because she *knew* what they needed to be.

❖   ❖   ❖

Ravin knew that he had the princess where he wanted her. He could see the anger in her. If she was anything like her sister or her brother, she would react to this ultimate insult, and one touch would be all it took. Let her aim one strike at him, and Ravin would have a way to cut her down with honor. At the very least, she would want to hurt him now, and commanders focused on that would not think clearly. He smiled slightly as he waited for her reply, calculating the insult in that as well as in the rest.

"I have a simple answer for you, King Ravin of the Southern Kingdom," Lenore said, and Ravin could appreciate her use of his old title.

"Consider before you say anything," Ravin said. "There is no second chance here."

"I am aware," Lenore said. "And now I must make an offer to *you*."

"An offer to me?" Ravin said, trying to hold back his surprise.

"Take your men, go back to your own kingdom. Withdraw from Royalsport at once and march directly to your ships. Do that, and you will be permitted to live, in spite of everything you have done to my family."

There was more steel in her voice than Ravin might have expected. He actually found himself admiring her a little for that.

"A pity," he said. "Go back to your lines, princess. I will kill you last, and when I kill you, your body will be displayed above my gates."

She shook her head. "When you die, you will not be displayed at all. You will be forgotten. All the achievements you hold so precious will fade away, and the world will realize that you have built nothing, *done* nothing that makes it better."

That was as sharp as her sister's blade had been. Ravin found himself admiring the girl then. She had become stronger than he could have imagined.

She turned to go, turning her back on him in a way that said that she wasn't scared of what might happen when she did it.

That was when Ravin heard the twang of a bow.

His eyes snapped around toward his own lines on instinct, and he saw a single shaft arcing out from the city walls, black against the sky. Ravin stared at it in horror, and it seemed to make its way across the sky at an almost leisurely pace, like some slender, deadly bird.

Ravin started to move, started to cry out a warning, which seemed an absurd thing to do for an enemy. He wasn't doing it for her though; he was doing it for himself. He was too late though, and saw the moment when it struck Lenore in the back, right where her heart would be.

She stumbled, and she fell, the impact knocking her down. Ravin had seen enough wounds in his time to know that this one would kill her before she hit the ground. The absurdity of it, the brutality, made him whirl back toward his lines.

"Which fool did that?" he bellowed. "I want him found! I want him *dead!*"

All the effort he'd put in to preserve the honor of this moment, to have it seen that he'd won this last victory the right way, and someone from his lines had *dared* to undo that with an arrow? It was *beyond* dishonor. If he'd cut Lenore down during a parley, that would have been bad enough, but at least it would have been seen as a matter between leaders, with Ravin being strong and direct. This ... this showed him as a coward!

Whoever had done it would take *days* to die, begging for an end to it.

Ravin's fury was almost absolute, but he still had the sense to spin back toward Lenore. He had no doubt that the battle lines on Lenore's side would already be advancing, ready to avenge their fallen leader. He could see all the ways that might play out, with the fury of their assault, the determination to get to him for vengeance.

Yet when he turned back, he *didn't* see the princess lying there dead on the cobbles. Instead, she was rising back to her feet, pulling the arrow from her back as she did so. Ravin saw the glint of steel there, and realized that she'd worn armor under her dress.

She turned back to him and started to back away. "So much for honor."

Ravin didn't bother trying to explain it. It didn't matter; what mattered was the look of the thing. He'd just been shown as a dishonorable foe, regardless of the truth of it. All that was left now was to return to his own lines, and he did so, stalking back there, joining the men who waited beyond the city walls. He felt his anger building up inside him. It was time to end this.

Away across the open ground before the city, Ravin heard horns and saw banners waving as Lenore shouted commands. She made her way back to the side of that monk of hers, and slowly, her army started to move forward. Ravin watched them for a moment or two, making sure that they were all moving in the ways that he had expected them to before he committed his own forces.

It was too late to think about honor now, too late for anything but victory. He held up a fist, and around him, men readied themselves.

Then he brought it down sharply, pointing at the enemy lines.

"Forward! Kill them all!"

CHAPTER TWENTY

O dd drew his blade, thinking about all the things that they could have done differently in the last few weeks, all the ways that it could have turned out another way. He shook his head; this was not the moment for thoughts like that. Instead, it was the moment for focus, and for battle.

"Forward," Lenore commanded. She didn't remount her horse, and to Odd that seemed like a good idea. It was a borrowed one, not trained for war, and there was too much risk of it panicking. "Give the order!"

"Forward!" Odd shouted, and the word was echoed down the line. Lenore was already starting for the enemy, taking up an arming sword as she went. Odd wished that he could argue with her about this part of the plan. Why did it need her to charge in with the rest of them? Why couldn't she wait here, and be seen by her forces?

He knew that he would never be able to persuade her, though. The most he could do was try to keep her alive through this.

"Forward!" he repeated. "Protect the queen!"

He started forward, keeping up with Lenore and then moving past her so that any man who tried to get to her would have to go through him first. Others started to move into place around him, and although Lenore had put most of the heavy troops provided by the three lords on the flanks to try to close in around the enemy, Odd had made sure that there was a core of hardened men here, armored in partial plate and carrying fine-edged blades, even if they'd put rags over them to blend in with the rest of the peasants. He would not allow her to be in danger.

Yet in battle, there was nowhere to hide from the danger. Odd could see threats all around. There was the danger that would come from the bulk of Ravin's toughest forces being at one end of his line. There was the chaos of the battle about to unfold, the enemy's greater numbers, a thousand and one things running through his mind.

"Shields!" he yelled as arrows darkened the skies. Around him, men raised those shields they had, ducking behind them as crossbow bolts and arrow shafts slammed into them. Their own archers started to lay down a withering barrage of their own, and one good thing about the way Ravin had set out his army was that it meant that their archers could keep up fire on the parts that were further away, while Ravin's had to hold fire to avoid hitting their own men. Lenore was still moving forward, but Odd made sure that a couple of men with strong shields got in front of her. He heard the thud of arrows against that wood, shafts stopped short of her.

Ravin's horse archers swept around in an arc to the flank, sending out a barrage of arrows, and Odd heard men scream as they went down. Lenore's forces had their own cavalry though, and the men there charged with spears raised to thrust, driving the horse archers back. Right then, Odd knew, the best protection was to keep moving forward. He felt the speed of the advance increase, but it was important to time the moment. Too early, and the energy of the rush would be spent. Too late, and the enemy could counterattack and overwhelm them.

"Wait," Odd commanded as they kept moving forward. "Wait... charge!"

He ran forward, keeping near Lenore, determined that she wouldn't be the one to bear the brunt of the first impact. Odd saw the enemy get closer and closer, then they were there, and all was screaming violence.

The clash of the two armies was like waves breaking against rocks, except that the impact was made of steel, and flesh, and violence. Men plunged onto spears, crying out with the impact, and those horsemen they had plunged lances down into the mass of their foes. Men cut and thrust and killed.

Odd slammed his shoulder into an enemy, feeling the impact as he smashed him back, cut out at another and sliced along the line of his shoulder. He smashed into the line of the enemy and through it.

His sword moved through a man's chest and came out again, smoothly, the sharpness of the blade making it almost... easy. In that moment, he was no longer thinking the thousand thoughts that had come before. He was no longer thinking about this or that tactic, about any of the things that they'd discussed with Greave. Instead, those thoughts gave way to something pure, something perfect. The meditative clarity fell on Odd in an instant, and he went with it, cutting into his foes with the pure beauty of death.

As the armies clashed, Greave could hear the screams of the dying, the bellows of anger and pain and frustration. He could hear the clatter of steel, built into a cacophony without any rhythm or reason to it. He'd read so many poems and tales that spoke about war, learned songs that sang of heroic exploits. All of them gave it a sense of order that wasn't there now, tried to make something neat out of... out of *this*.

His hands twitched in frustration as he stood with Erin out in one of the fields beyond the city, close to the edge of the forest. He wasn't a warrior, yet even so, he felt as if he should be doing something.

Erin was worse. She had her spear out, and looked as if she would charge forward to join in the battle at the slightest chance. When the arrow had struck Lenore, Greave had actually had to grab her arm to stop her charging forward. He didn't do it now, but he did step slightly in front of her, just in case.

"We have to wait," Greave said. "You know we do."

"I know," Erin said. "That doesn't mean I have to *like* it, though."

"I don't like it either," Greave said. "I don't like Lenore being in danger and not being able to help."

"You have helped," Erin said. "You *are* helping."

It was hard to believe it though when he could see and hear so many dying. He saw whole lines of men seem to go down, saw spears and swords plunge into flesh, saw violence on such a scale that it was almost impossible to think of any individual part of it.

He saw one man standing over another, smashing down again and again with the edge of a shield. He saw that man brought down by the swing of an axe, only for *that* man to be swallowed up by the flow of the battle. He saw another man fighting what seemed like a duel in a brief empty space, only for both men in that fight to be ridden down by a horse without a rider, its owner already fallen.

He could see Lenore at the heart of it all, wearing her dress over her armor, surrounded by her own troops. She stood out because of the way she was dressed, like a jewel shining out in a sea of mud and blood and death. Greave knew that it was a deliberate choice, trying to draw Ravin's men away from their leader's plans with the urge to get to her, but even so, it terrified him that she was putting herself in danger like that.

Even as Greave watched, a man ran straight at Lenore with a sword raised, making his heart tighten in his chest for the second or so it took before Odd stepped in the way and cut the man down with a double-handed stroke.

"I want to kill them," Erin said. "I want to kill them all."

Greave could see her anger, and he could understand it. A part of him wanted to do exactly the same. He wanted to charge in, wanted to help Lenore. He hated the way he had to stand there, unable to join the fight.

At the same time, he knew that it wasn't the way for him to help. He couldn't delude himself into thinking that he could wade in and defeat the enemy singlehanded. He wasn't Erin. *His* skills lay in knowledge and thinking, in being able to treat even something like this like a gigantic puzzle.

To do that, though, he needed to stop thinking about the individual moments of the battle. It was like looking at a flock of birds and trying to stare at each one rather than understanding the flow of the whole. It was a way to get too caught up to really see anything of use.

It took an effort of will for Greave to pull back his attention from the violence of the battle. His family didn't need someone right then who could feel empathy for the agony of a horse having its legs cut from under it, or wonder at a man still fighting with half a dozen arrows sticking from his flesh. They needed someone who could look past the chaos to the units beyond, the pressures and the tactics.

It took several seconds to see it now that the armies were engaged with one another. Slowly though, he found that he could see it. Greave could see where the strongest units of Ravin's army were pressing against those on the left flank of Lenore's, could see the danger as Ravin's skir-mishers moved in to support them.

Now, he could see it all like pieces of the whole, could see the dangers and the possibilities, understand the flow of the whole. He'd read so many books on strategy and the art of war over the years, and it had all seemed so unpleasant and abstract to him, more Rodry's domain than his.

Now, he saw the reality of it, saw the application of simple maxims about forcing enemies to engage, then striking elsewhere, about using the smallest textures of the landscape to advantage.

He thought about the ways he might use that to his advantage, about the orders he might give, and the things he might do to help. He couldn't do that, though. That wasn't why he was here. Ravin would have some kind of plan, and it was Greave's job to work out what it was.

Before it killed his sister, and all of them.

CHAPTER TWENTY ONE

Aurelle was the one who saw Renard first, running in toward the House of Sighs, big and red-haired, far too obvious to ever succeed as well as he had as a thief. She'd been looking out her window for a spell, watching out for dangers to the House of Sighs. With an army outside the city, and Ravin's forces mobilized, Royalsport could become a very dangerous place in the next few hours.

Part of the reason she was looking out was that she was half expecting Duke Viris to send for her. She thought that she'd done a good job, whispering the right words to him, reminding him that his ambition had been for his son to rule, not to be a lackey. Sooner or later in a situation like this, he would send for her with some task to advance his cause, and Aurelle would have to decide the best thing to do for the kingdom.

For now though, there was Renard. Aurelle hurried down through the House, to the door that was closest to the line he was hurrying on. She heard the arguing before she even reached it.

"But when you left, Lady Meredith *said*—" the young man at the door began.

"I don't care what she said!" Renard bellowed back. "I need to come back in and talk to her. It's a matter of life and death."

Aurelle reached the doorway, where Renard was arguing with one of the door attendants. He looked as if he might be about to shove his way past, and that would only end in violence. Those who served the doors might not look threatening, but all were skilled with hidden weapons.

"Enough," Aurelle said gently to the door guard. "This is not meant to be a place of shouting. Would Lady Meredith approve of this?"

"No," the door attendant agreed. "But still, she told him to get out of her House. She clearly doesn't want to see him."

Aurelle raised an eyebrow. "Is anything ever that clear with Lady Meredith? And with the two of them together, I suspect that things get very muddied indeed."

The young man nodded his assent, but Aurelle was already turning her attention to Renard.

"And you, how is it that you've ever managed to sneak in anywhere, with the noise you make?"

Renard looked a little ashamed at that.

"Come on," Aurelle said to him. "I'll take you up to Lady Meredith."

She led the way up through the House, and Renard looked as if he were ready to burst.

"I thought you were getting Erin out of the city," she said.

Renard nodded. "I did. That's why I'm here. I ... no, I need to explain all this once."

Aurelle could understand that, but even so there was something about the way Renard hurried through the House that made her want to know everything that he had to say.

They found Meredith in her rooms, giving instructions to member after member of it. They filed in one at a time, and she whispered to them, and they hurried off. Aurelle was surprised by it; not by the fact that Meredith was doing it, but that she was doing it so indiscreetly, with a whole line of those who served there waiting, when usually they would have been summoned more subtly.

Meredith looked up as Aurelle brought Renard in. She frowned. "You're back?"

"I couldn't stay away from your—" Renard began.

"If the next word out of your mouth is 'beauty,'" Meredith said, "I will have you thrown out of a very high window."

Aurelle smiled at that slightly, wondering if Meredith would actually do it. Renard seemed taken aback for a moment, but seemed to recover quickly. He started to do the one thing that almost never happened here, in this place, and started to talk openly.

"I took Princess Erin out of the city," he said, "and we found...we found Lenore. She was out there with an army, it's her army attacking the city, and there are components from at least three or four lords, some peasants..."

He was talking quickly enough that there wasn't even time to scatter all the people from the room who didn't need to hear this. To Aurelle, he seemed to be in such a rush that he couldn't stop himself, the words just pouring out like a waterfall, barely leaving enough space for him to take a breath.

"They have a plan to win, but it needs all of our help. Prince Greave says—"

"Greave?" Aurelle said, unable to stop herself. "Greave is *dead.*"

Renard turned to her. "Aurelle, I'm so sorry. I should have told you the moment I came in. Prince Greave is alive. I met him myself in the camp. He traveled to the city and found his sister's army waiting. He has come up with a plan to defeat Ravin. He's out there now, with the army."

Feelings flashed through Aurelle so quickly that it was hard to keep up with them. First, there was disbelief, the certainty that Renard had to be lying as part of some scheme, or that the man claiming to be Greave had to be some kind of imposter, because she'd seen him die...

But what had she seen? She'd seen the flames on the docks, seen the structure of them collapse. She'd thought that no one could have survived that, but what...what if Greave had? What if he'd somehow thought of a way to live through it? What if he'd come back all this way?

Some part of that must have shown on her face, because Renard put a hand on her shoulder. "I promise you, it's him. His sisters were there, and Erin almost fell over, she was so shocked at seeing him."

Hope came next; hope that this might actually be true, that Greave might actually be out there. He'd come to Royalsport, the city where he'd sent her. Did that mean...no, she didn't dare to hope for *that*; he'd probably come back looking for his family. Even so, the fact that he was alive meant everything to Aurelle in that moment. Everything.

Guilt came next, that she hadn't looked harder for him after Astare, that she hadn't forced the captain to turn his boat around. She'd had to kill him anyway in the end, so why couldn't she have done it then? Why couldn't she have been there for him?

That just left fear. Fear, because he was out there in danger now, while she was in here. He was out in a battle, and the middle of a battle was no place for a man like Greave. With blades and arrows on all sides, it would be only too easy for one of them to find Greave's heart, and for Aurelle's to break all over again. No, she wouldn't find him again only to lose him. She needed to find him, needed to get to him before the battle could swallow up the sweet, gentle man she loved.

She started for the door, and Meredith was in front of her then.

"Aurelle," she said, putting her hands on Aurelle's shoulders. "Aurelle, stop."

"Get out of my way," Aurelle said.

"Aurelle, you have to think," Meredith said.

A gasp went around the room, and Aurelle realized that without thinking about it, she'd drawn a knife. Half a dozen other people were reaching for their own weapons. She saw Meredith make a gesture, waving them away.

"I know you want to go to him," Meredith said. "I know you want to save him. There's a battle in the way, Aurelle. Are you going to fight your way through all of it to get to your prince?"

"If I have to," Aurelle snarled.

"You'll die, and it won't do anything to help him," Meredith said. "You are the best at striking from the shadows, but in a battle, there are none. You can't help him by charging in. Come on, Aurelle. I trained you to think."

That was true; think first, act when necessary. This was just raw action, driven by emotion. The worst part was that Meredith was right: there was no way that she could get through the middle of a battle to help Greave. She hadn't felt so helpless since ... since watching what she'd thought was his death on the docks, back in Astare.

"I need to do something," Aurelle said. She put her knife away.

"And I'm sure Renard has brought something for us to do," Meredith said, calmly. "Something urgent, if he's bursting in here and babbling important things like a child who doesn't know how to keep a secret."

She looked over to Renard pointedly, and Aurelle looked too.

"We need to act in the city during the battle," Renard said. "We need to get as many to rise up as we can. Not just nobles; all the people. All the things you've been planning, Meredith. *This* is the moment for it."

"Yes," Meredith said. "I know."

"You *know*?" Renard said, sounding faintly amazed.

"This House can collect the subtlest of information, find out things no one else can," Meredith pointed out. "And yet you're acting as if I don't have eyes. Did you think I wouldn't notice a *battle* outside the walls of the city?" She gestured to the people already there in the room. "Everyone here has their orders."

"You might need to change some of them to account for Prince Greave's plan," Renard said. He moved in to whisper to Meredith. Even as close as she was, Aurelle couldn't hear the words.

"I see," Meredith said. "Most of what I have in place should suffice. Aurelle, will you play your part in this? We need you, if we're going to get the city to rise up. You can't help out there, but here, you could change *everything.*"

"I..." Aurelle still wanted to find a way to get to Greave, but she knew that there was no way. The way to see him again was to hope. Hope that this all worked, hope that they won, hope that she could see him in an aftermath where they'd defeated their foes. To get to that, though, she had to play her part.

"I guess I have no choice," she said.

Chapter Twenty Two

O dd plunged into the heart of the battle, his longsword gripped in both hands. Savage clarity gripped him, halfway between the purity of meditation and the fury of battle rage, like a beast on a careful leash. He ran through the battle, striking as he went.

All the techniques that he'd learned in his years as a knight came out as effortlessly as breathing. He cut into a foe's parry, changed the angle as he stepped off to the side, and cut down behind him as he ran past. He saw a spear coming in from the side, and barely deflected it in time. He moved on without stopping to cut down the man who had struck at him.

This was a real battle. The fight in the House of Weapons when he'd stood back to back with Swordmaster Wendros had been one thing, but this was another entirely. This wasn't just foes on every side, it was more foes than Odd could hope to count, with men pressing together, weapons coming in almost out of nowhere.

Battles made a mockery of skill. The sheer numbers of foes meant that a blade could come at any time, from any angle. The pressure of them could slow the fastest fighter to a halt, wear down the stamina of the strongest. Odd had seen the bravest, finest men brought down in such places, when they could have felled almost any foe in a duel.

There were two ways to fight in such a place. One was to stand shoulder to shoulder with allies, watching out for one another, and relying on armor to protect from the blows that no one could hope to stop.

The other way was … this. The clarity that Odd held to seemed to push him into a space where skill *could* matter. Odd charged through the battlefield, flowed through it, never stopped moving even for a moment. To stop was to die. To engage too long with one foe was to be struck down by another he couldn't see, so he threw himself forward, cutting when he saw openings, deflecting blades that came at his head, dancing through the chaos of it, *being* the chaos of it.

He cut men down like a farmer cutting corn. He caught a blade against his sword's cross-guard, let go with one hand, and grabbed the pommel of his foe's sword to wrench it to the side, opening the way for him to thrust his sword home.

On it went, and on, even though it had probably been only minutes so far. For the briefest moment in the battle, Odd found himself in a clear space, able to look around. He saw men on every side of him, cutting and killing. What he *couldn't* see was Lenore. Somewhere in the rush of his advance, he'd lost her.

Odd felt a moment of panic. He'd sworn to protect her, and yet now he'd left her side in the midst of a battle. It didn't matter that she had protectors around her, or that Odd could do plenty of good just by attacking. Odd peered out through the battle, looking for a flash of her dress, a glimpse of her face.

Needing to find her, he plunged back in, dropping back into the clarity of the fight, starting to kill again as he sought her.

Sir Frederick Narretz stood on the left of the battle, trying to hold back the press of some of Emperor Ravin's strongest troops, struggling and pushing as much as striking with his sword. He felt blows rattle against his armor, feeling lucky that he had a knight's plate rather than the simple leathers or padding of most of those who fought.

He found space to strike out at one of those in front of him, and felt a certain grim satisfaction as the man fell. He had spent most of his life believing that service to his lord was the thing that mattered most. He'd done all that Lord Carrick had commanded, no matter how unpleasant, because he'd thought that honor had demanded it.

Then Lenore had come to Lord Carrick's castle, and he'd seen how wrong he was. Now he knew what it was to fight for a cause that mattered, and Frederick was determined to do all that he could.

He cut again into the mass of men in front of him, lifting his shield to block a blow in return. This close, all he could do was keep battering at the men in front of him, trying to thrust with the point to find gaps in the armor of his enemies.

Briefly, he found himself in open space, the suddenness of the press opening out sending Frederick whirling, unsure which line was which. He saw a man in scale armor in front of him and lunged forward, thrusting his arming sword toward a gap in the man's armor.

His foe turned, parrying the blow with a curved sword and then slashing back toward Frederick. He caught the strike on his shield, angling it to deflect the blow, and trying to cut back simultaneously. His opponent dodged back from the attack, though, leaving Sir Frederick cutting at air.

The other soldier raised his sword high and then leapt forward, cutting down. At the last minute, he pulled back to dodge the strike Sir Frederick threw in response, cutting again in the aftermath.

Frederick had seen that trick before, though, and was already raising his shield to block the stroke, ducking down beneath it like a man holding a clock over his head during a rainstorm. This time, as he thrust up with his blade, he felt it plunge through the chest of his foe. He forced his way back up to his feet, close as a lover as he tried to drag his blade clear of the other man's chest.

That was when pain exploded in his side, burning and cold, all at once.

Frederick turned his head and saw a second swordsman there, coming out of the mass of the battle. Frederick tried to strike a blow back at him, but his arm had no strength left in it. It felt so unfair, so arbitrary, and yet all around him, Frederick could see men being cut down.

He held to the foe he'd killed, and they sagged down to the ground together. As he gasped his last breaths, the battle washed over him.

Ravin led the charge of his men, encased in his armor, letting blows slide off it while he struck great two-handed blows with Heartsplitter. He all but cut a man in half, lanced the tip of it through another's guts, and moved on, leaving him screaming.

He smashed aside a peasant swinging an axe at him, felt the impact of a sword against his armor, and turned to see a farmer trying to wind up for another blow. He cut the man's head from his shoulders in a single sweep, then brought his blade back just in time to stop a pitchfork aimed at his guts.

Men fell around him. One of his soldiers died with a sword hacking into his chest, another spun as an arrow slammed into him. Ravin snatched up a shield from a fallen soldier, raising it in time to block a couple of crossbow bolts and then slamming the edge into the skull of another opponent.

Cutting through them felt almost too easy. There were knights in some parts of Princess Lenore's forces, but here it seemed to be peasants and lightly armored woodsmen. They were hardly worthy foes for a man like him. Even as he thought it, Ravin kicked a man out of his way, stepped into the gap, and cut through another's arm.

Ravin found himself thinking about the girl who had come at him in the night: Princess Erin. She had come as close as anyone in recent times to actually killing him. Ravin had no false modesty about his skills; he was big, and strong, and dangerously fast with it. He'd been killing men for most of his life, and had skills with the sword that could match any sword master. Yet the girl had come close to striking him down.

Ravin looked around the battlefield for her. She would be out there somewhere; she wouldn't be able to keep away.

Greave was finding it harder and harder to keep hold of his sister's arm.

"This has to be the moment!" Erin said. "*Look* at it, Greave!"

Greave was watching, and the more he watched the battle, the more concerned he was becoming. He could see the way that Ravin's forces were scything into the weakest parts of Lenore's forces, could see his sister surrounded by a small core of her stronger troops, drawing in the violence of the rest.

The left was collapsing, where Ravin's most armored troops were pressing into some of those retainers the lords had given Lenore. The right, where there were more of those better troops, was struggling to swing around to aid the rest in time, and by doing so, it was exposing its flank to Ravin's weaker skirmishers, who could do damage against troops who weren't so well protected now.

It all pointed to one thing: they were losing.

"We have to get involved," Erin said. "Lenore could be dying in there, Greave."

She wrenched out of his grasp and took a step toward the battle.

"Erin," Greave said. "Do you think I don't want to be there? Do you think I don't want to charge forward and try to save our sister? You know more about violence than I ever could. In a sword fight, do you throw wild attacks at every target? Or do you wait for the moment to strike?"

"You know the answer to that," Erin said. "But what happens if you wait so long that your opponent has already stabbed you in the heart?"

That was the hardest part of all of it. Greave had to stand there and watch, trusting in the plan they'd made, trusting that everything would work out the way he'd set it out. He had to do that, even while he saw men cut down on every side of the field, and while he saw Lenore's forces pressed back, folded in, forced to give ground. He wanted to trust that everything would work out, but for now…

…now, they were losing, and if Greave waited too long, they might be wiped out completely.

CHAPTER TWENTY THREE

V ars followed Bethe as she moved from person to person out on the streets beyond her home, their home.

"What's going on?" Bethe asked another of her neighbors. "Do you know what's happening?"

Vars wasn't comfortable being out there. He wanted to be back inside her little wood and daub house, wanted to be out of sight. With an army out in front of the city, it made more sense to hide away and wait, with an escape route carefully planned, yet Bethe seemed to want to be there, moving from person to person, always asking the same questions.

"This isn't helping, Bethe," Vars said, but she was already moving to the next neighbor, the next rumor.

So far, it was *all* rumors, the people of their district making guesses and spreading them like … well, like the dragon fire that had ripped through the city before. The lords had risen up in rebellion, it wasn't an army, but bandits come to pillage, or a horde of those fleeing violence elsewhere, Godwin was risen from the dead to bring an army … Vars flinched at the last of those.

"We should go back inside," he said to Bethe. "It doesn't *matter* who's attacking, or who wins. If Ravin's army wins, they'll plunder through the city again in celebration. If the others win, then even if they're trying to save the city, their troops will still hurt anyone who gets in the way."

"Not everyone is like that," Bethe insisted.

Vars wanted to argue that people were *always* like that. That they put themselves first and others nowhere. That those with power hurt those without, and that they didn't really help one another if it meant any danger to them. He wanted to say all those things, but Bethe was like living

114

proof that it wasn't true. She was so much better than him that it was like ... like he *wanted* the world to be the way she saw it.

"It still might not be safe," Vars said.

"I'll go back once I know what's really going on," Bethe said. They kept walking through the district, chatting with their neighbors, as if answers would appear if they all worked on them enough.

They were still doing it when more came out into the streets, armed with what looked like any weapon they'd been able to find, shouting three words over and over.

"For the queen! For the queen!"

These were ordinary looking people, armed with knives and hammers, lengths of wood and cleavers. For the first few instants, Vars's instinct was to run from them, because it would be easy for a group like that to turn into a mob, but Bethe wasn't running. Instead, she walked *toward* them. She actually reached out for one of them, touching his arm to bring him to a halt.

"What's going on?" she asked. "What do you know?"

"The army outside belongs to Queen Lenore!" the man replied, the excitement in his voice obvious. It wasn't excitement that Vars felt, though. It was fear, disbelief, shock, shame, all mingled together until he didn't know what to think or say.

"Are you sure?" he blurted. "Are you sure it's Lenore?"

"*Queen* Lenore," the man replied. Others were still striding past, spreading out in the streets, encouraging others to go get weapons. "And plenty of us saw it with our own eyes. She stepped out to meet Ravin alone, leaving her mad monk back with her armies. They say ... they say that she offered Ravin the chance to surrender, and he had her shot with an arrow while her back was turned."

That made a surprising emotion rise in Vars: fear for his sister. It was something he would have never imagined feeling. It wasn't as if he'd ever really cared for his half-siblings, or even for his brothers. Yet now, he felt his heart tighten in his chest.

"She ... she's dead?" he said.

"Of course she isn't," the other man replied, as if the idea that Lenore might be dead were some kind of heresy. "She knew that he would try to betray her, and she wore armor. She walked back to her army, condemning him for a truce breaker, and commanded her forces to charge."

Vars wasn't sure how much to believe of this, given the other rumors that were flying around among his neighbors. Still, it felt as if there might be a grain of truth to this as there hadn't been for so much of the rest of it.

"So why are you all out here?" Bethe asked while Vars was still trying to make some kind of sense of it.

The man she'd stopped looked at them like it was obvious. "We're going to take control of the streets," he said. "People from the House of Sighs came around, telling us that the city needs us, and they're right. This is our moment! This is when we throw off the southerners' control."

Vars could see the excitement in Bethe almost instantly. She turned to him, determined.

"This is our chance," she said. "Come on."

She started to head back toward her house, fast enough that Vars had to hurry to keep up.

"What are you planning?" he asked.

"I'm going to join them," Bethe said. "We have to. It's our best chance to make things better."

"Or the best way to get killed," Vars pointed out.

Bethe was already at the door to her house, and went inside. Vars followed, trying to think of a way to talk her out of this. It seemed obvious that he should. Plunging into the middle of a fight was not the way for Bethe to stay safe, and he *wanted* her to stay safe. Talking about going out onto the streets to fight against the invaders was easy enough, but actually doing it might kill her, kill both of them.

"Bethe," Vars said, "you can't really be thinking of doing this."

"Why not?" Bethe asked. She snatched up a long cooking knife and a thick rolling pin. "Everyone is gathering to help with this. I want to be a part of it. I want to *do* something, Vars."

"Then do the sensible thing," Vars said. "Stay here, stay *safe*."

"What are you afraid of?" Bethe demanded.

Vars laughed bitterly at that. "*Everything.*" It felt strange to admit it, but Bethe felt like the one person he could admit it to. The one person he didn't *have* to pretend to be brave around. "All my life, I've been afraid of everything. I'm a coward, Bethe."

"You saved me," she pointed out.

"I was looking for a way to run!" Vars shouted, and instantly felt ashamed. He looked to Bethe, expecting to see her hatred there, her disgust at him. Instead, he saw sympathy, and the same determination from before.

"You *didn't* run," Bethe said. "You fought them. You should fight *now*. It's all right to be afraid, Vars, if you do the right thing."

"And what about when Ravin wins the battle, and his Quiet Men take anyone who was involved in fighting back?" Vars argued. "What about if the army outside wins, and it turns out that it's *not* Lenore, but some lord whose response to ordinary folk rising up will be to treat them as enemies to be killed?"

"What about if we could succeed in this, but because I don't play my part, it doesn't happen?" Bethe countered. She took a step toward the door.

"Do you really think that one person can make any kind of difference?" Vars asked. "Why not let everyone else do this?"

"And what if everyone felt like that?" Bethe asked. "Maybe I can't change things all by myself, but a hundred people, a thousand, *can* do something."

"Please, Bethe," Vars begged, and he'd never begged for anything that wasn't his own life before. "I just want you to be safe."

Vars heard her sigh.

"Look," she said, "you stay here if you want. You *hide* here if you want, but I'm not going to sit in the house and do nothing when there's a chance to do something about the men who killed my husband."

Vars knew then that she was serious, and that there was nothing he could say that would dissuade her. Bethe had a kind of steel in her that he'd never had, although now he found himself wishing that he had it, wishing that he had the strength to fight like her.

"All right," he said. "I'll come. But there has to be a better way to do it than this."

"Like what?" Bethe asked.

Vars tried to think. He might not be the great thinker that his brother Greave was, or have Rodry's knack for battle, but when it came to sneaking and cunning, there were few better. Vars was surprised to feel shame at that, but at least now it could be put to good use. He thought, and thought...

An idea came to him, sudden as dawn.

"We take the castle," he said. "Ravin has taken his men out to fight. With the battles in the streets, more will go out to try to control them. The castle will be virtually unguarded."

"Even at a time like this, you're thinking about trying to take your throne back?" Bethe demanded. She sounded shocked, and more than a little disappointed.

"No," Vars said. "I don't want the castle for myself. I don't want to be king." It was strange, realizing the truth of it as he said it. The kingdom did not need King Vars, not again. "But we can hold it for whoever is attacking. If it's Lenore, we give it to her, and we make sure that Ravin has nowhere to retreat."

"That's... maybe it makes sense," Bethe admitted.

"Think about it," Vars insisted. "Think about the way my family fell back to the castle, then to the keep. Ravin has the men to hold both, and he won't have someone like me betraying him." Again, he had to ignore the wash of shame. "So our best option is to deny him the castle in the first place. And if the attackers *aren't* with Lenore, if it's all some trick, we'll have leverage to make them treat the people here better."

"Does that actually matter to you?" Bethe asked.

Vars thought about lying, but this seemed like a moment for truth, especially with her. "Honestly, I'm not sure. But it matters to you, and what you want matters to me."

He watched as Bethe thought a little longer. "All right," she said. "I'll see if I can convince people out there to join us. We have a castle to retake."

CHAPTER TWENTY FOUR

R avin fought at the heart of the battle, blood covering the gold of his armor by now, feeling a savage joy as he forced his foes back step by step. Soon, the victory would be his, and the last of his foes would fall. Soon, the kingdom would be his without question.

He deflected a short sword and slammed Heartsplitter's hilt into a man's face, feeling the crunch of bone. He lopped the head from a thrusting spear, and briefly he found himself thinking of Princess Erin again. He hoped that she was in the press of the battle somewhere; he would enjoy killing her.

For now, he had to settle for the meager offerings in front of him. A peasant came at him with a scythe; Ravin hacked him down. Another swung an axe, and Ravin shoved him into a waiting mass of his troops almost contemptuously.

It wasn't that it was easy, because no battle truly was. Already, Ravin had a dozen scratches and scrapes from glancing blows, or where his armor had dug into his skin as it had protected him. He could feel the sapping effort of it all too, because true battle was enough to tax even a man like him.

Yet at the same time, there were no *true* foes for him here. Even a man in full plate who came at him did so slowly, without the speed to get through Ravin's defenses. Ravin battered the first blow aside, turned his shoulder to take the impact of a shield, and hooked his leg behind his foe's to send him tumbling to the ground.

For an instant, Ravin stumbled, and he drove up to his feet with all the determination of a man seeking to avoid drowning. A battle was no place to fall, and even with the speed that he rose he took a kick to the ribs. He all but decapitated the man who had struck him, and saw the would be knight struggling to rise. Ravin reversed his blade and plunged it down through him with a roar.

"Will no one worthy face me?" he bellowed.

Not that it truly mattered. Ravin was an intelligent man; he knew that victory was what mattered, and that wishing for more dangerous foes was a fool's dream. Still, he wanted better than this... dross.

He could still feel satisfaction as they gave ground, though. His men were folding up their lines, little by little, and although they were holding for now, it was only a matter of time, especially when his reinforcements came into the fray.

Briefly, he glimpsed Lenore through the battle, standing resplendent even though her dress was torn to reveal the armor beneath. He thought of heading for her and finishing things, but no, not yet. He would have *something* to savor in this battle. More than that, he needed something to wipe away the story of an arrow shot during a truce. He needed an end for her so terrible that it would eclipse even that. He would kill her last, making her watch every man and woman who had put their trust in her die. Then... well, her death would be a thing of horror.

Merl flinched at the horror of the violence around him, barely parrying an axe blow and stabbing out randomly with his messer. *This* wasn't like robbing a few folk out on the roads, where the worse that happened was fighting a few at a time, most of whom didn't know anything about weapons. *Now* he was in the press of the violence, trying to hold back waves of Ravin's soldiers.

All because he'd listened to Lenore. As another weapon came toward his head, a part of Merl told him that he'd been stupid, that he should have run in the face of Sir Odd, not agreed to sign up to Lenore's mad cause. He didn't quite deflect the impact of a sword, feeling it scrape down his shoulder, the pain of it sharp and sudden. Merl struck back frantically, and his opponent fell away.

He had a moment then to look into the battle. He saw Queen Lenore's general, Sir Odd, moving through the battle like a whirlwind, wild and impossible to follow for more than a moment or two. His sword seemed to be leading him as he fought, so that the movement of his body behind it was a mere afterthought. He fought in a wave of violence that seemed to break over all around him, sword taking a head from a body, slicing open an opponent through the gaps in his armor. He looked as if there was nowhere else in the world he belonged more.

Merl *didn't* belong. He didn't want to be here, he *hated* being here. And yet... yet there was nowhere else that meant more for him to be right then. He'd been nothing out on the roads. At least here he had the chance to do something that *meant* something, something *good.*

Even as he thought it, Merl saw a peasant boy knocked down, a soldier standing over him. Merl charged for him without thinking about it, swinging his sword at the man's throat, reaching out an arm to try to intercept the sword before it could drop. He missed his grab on the arm, and felt agony as his finger caught hold of the blade instead, the sharpness of it cutting into him.

He thrust his own blade through the other man's neck, bringing him down in a spray of blood even as he doubled over clutching at his injured hand. He grinned at the peasant boy, helping him up to his feet and sending him plunging back into the fight.

Odd walked the balance between pure beauty and incandescent violence, both in harmony now as he cut and thrust, moved and killed. At this point, it had gone beyond the beauty of meditation, beyond battle rage, becoming something new. Odd saw the battle as moment after moment, movement after movement, and even as he *saw* he moved.

He cut out at a throat, spun in place and thrust his blade back through a man's chest. He swayed aside from a sword cut, then stepped in between two spears, pulling at one to send one man stumbling into the other.

Dimly, he was aware of something else pulsing beneath the violence and harmony, something pulling at him on the edge of his consciousness. Odd reached for it, but even as he did so, a knife scraped across his flank, the pain drawing him back just a little. The fury took control for a moment then, anger at being wounded even slightly driving him to cut up, slicing his foe from hip to shoulder, then back across at his head, his legs.

Odd struck and struck, and now it was hard for him to pick out one opponent from another. He turned his guard to deflect one sword, wound his way around another blade, shifted from posture to posture with his sword held high, then low, then pointed out at his foes.

For a moment or two, he teetered on the edge of full fury, barely able to contain his battle rage. He knew that if he gave in to it, he would kill friends as well as foes, completely indiscriminately.

One thought kept him from that: a simple image of a village on fire, the inhabitants slaughtered at his hands. He knew what this could do, and he would not be that man again.

That was enough for him to regain his balance, and Odd threw himself back into the fight. Around him, men died. Man after man came at him, or rather, found themselves pushed into Odd's path, because those with any choice about it fell out of his way, choosing any fight other than the one with him.

Odd took the briefest of breaths, and in that second, he saw Lenore again, caught up at the heart of the fight. Taking up his sword once more, he started to cut his way toward her.

Vilim was still reeling from almost being killed. He'd been down on the ground, a man about to stab him, and had only been saved when a man who'd looked like a bandit had come in to cut the man down. He'd hauled Vilim to his feet and then gone back into the chaos of the battle, leaving him alone.

He was so muddy that his normally pale hair was brown with it, his clothes crusted with it and with blood. He hadn't been able to find proper armor, so it had just been a question of strapping as many layers of padding and leather to himself as he could. Now, he sweltered in the heat of the fight.

Vilim wasn't sure what to do. He stood there, holding a sword that felt nothing like the stick he'd practiced with back on the farm, watching men fight and die around him. Blood sprayed over his face, and it was only as he turned that he saw that a man had been killed next to him.

He'd thought that this would be so simple: march with the queen, regain her throne and be a hero rather than a farm hand like his father. He'd thought that fights would be like something out of stories, rather than something that seemed to make no sense, filled with apparently random death on every side.

He hadn't even used his sword yet except in his brief, failed fight with the man who'd almost killed him. Instead, he stood there blindly, while the battle seemed to flow around him, uncaring.

Then another of Ravin's troops took notice of him, and smiled a cruel smile as he came forward, blade raised to sweep down.

Vilim wanted to run, wanted to throw down his sword and just flee. Instead, he found himself moving forward to meet the other man, some half memory of his lessons on the farm where they'd trained bringing his blade up to block the descending blow. It clattered against his blade and tore it from his grip.

There was no art to what Vilim did next. Rather than thinking about swordplay, he flung himself at the other man, bringing them both down in a heap, his wrist clamped on the soldier's sword arm. He fought now the way he might have fought outside a tavern, with fists and knees and elbows, hitting with anything he could to try to keep his opponent down. Blows thudded into his flesh, and they hurt, but Vilim knew he couldn't stop.

He managed to get a hand to the small knife he carried at his belt. He saw the soldier's eyes widen at the flash of it, and then Vilim was stabbing, again and again, until his foe went still beneath him.

He'd just killed a man.

The thought came to him with sickening force. It was nothing like he'd thought, with nothing heroic about it, only the need to kill before he was killed. Worse, in the melee there was no time to think about it, or to deal with the roiling sickness in his stomach. Instead, Vilim reached out, snatching up the other man's sword and hefting it, ready to fight again.

Even as he did so, a low sound came over the battlefield, deep and rolling. A horn sounded, and Vilim had no idea what it portended.

CHAPTER TWENTY FIVE

To Greave, the sound of the horn booming out across the battlefield was like the cry of some great beast, promising destruction.

"That's not one of ours," Erin said beside him.

"No," Greave agreed. It was coming from the city, rather than from their side of the battlefield, a single sonorous note repeated every few seconds.

"They're doing something," Erin said. "We have to act."

"We have to wait to see *what* they're doing," Greave insisted. "What is the first rule of battle?"

"That there *are* no rules, and you stab the other bastard until they stop trying to kill you," Erin replied. She smiled as Greave gave her an exasperated look. "I learned to fight from the mad knight, remember?"

"Erin," Greave insisted. "What's the biggest advantage in battle?"

"Aside from 'more troops'?" Erin countered, but then stopped herself. "Knowing your enemy."

Greave nodded. "And what do we know about Ravin?"

"Is this really the moment for one of your lectures, Greave?" Erin asked.

It was, if it could hold her back a few more seconds when she might otherwise have been charging into the fight without a thought. Even in trying to slow down his sister, it paid to think.

"Indulge me," Greave said.

"That he plans ahead. That he sees things coming," Erin said. Greave saw her wince, and he guessed that the memories of her attempt to kill the emperor were uncomfortable in that moment. Or maybe it was just her injuries. "He likes to set things up and then crush people when they've blundered into his trap."

"Exactly," Greave said. "So we have to let his trap unfold."

That wasn't an easy thing to say, when below, people on their side were still dying. As much as Greave tried to keep himself focused on the bigger picture, he couldn't keep from seeing a man crawling through the churned up field, his stomach opened, couldn't stop from staring at a woman stabbed through by a spear, trying to drag herself along its length to get to the soldier who'd struck her before she died.

Even pulling back his focus from the individual fights, it was bad, because Greave could see exactly how much ground Lenore's forces had given up, exactly how many lines and mounds of bodies there now were where groups of soldiers had made stands only to be cut down. It pained him just to see it.

Maybe that was another reason his sister had given him the job she had: because she'd known that Greave would be able to look on all this pain and suffering and still do the job he'd been given. That didn't make it any easier, though.

"When this is done," he said, "I will write a ballad about the horrors of this day, and I'll write it truly, so that no one will want to go into battle again."

"It's a nice thought," Erin replied. "But it won't work. People don't like songs that tell them the truth. They'll listen to the other ones."

"What other ones?"

"About heroes cutting down all before them," Erin said. She pointed to the tiny speck of a figure in the remains of monastic robes, leaving a swath of bodies behind. "About beautiful princesses." She pointed to Lenore, still at the heart of the battle. She pointed to Greave. "About Prince Greave the Patient, who waited his foes to death."

"Soon," Greave promised. "Soon, Erin."

Ravin's forces seemed to be moving now. Their pressure on the left of Lenore's army had been relentless, but now they seemed to be pulling back a fraction in response to the horn. If Lenore's men had been fresh, it might have been a good moment to strike at them, but this far into the battle, there was no way to make a move like that work. Instead, those of Lenore's soldiers who weren't caught up in desperate fights seemed to be taking a second to catch their breath, or maybe steeling themselves for whatever renewed onslaught was to come.

At first, Greave thought that Ravin might be forming a line in front of the city, daring Lenore's troops to come on and falter against them like waves breaking on rocks. Yet Greave could see the shape of that line too, the strongest troops of Ravin's forces placing themselves toward the center now. This wasn't a line designed to absorb an attack; it was one that would become a wedge when it charged again, smashing into the heart of Lenore's forces.

Even while Ravin's forces did so, Greave saw Lenore's people trying to form up again, those who could resuming positions ready to meet the attack. Greave saw Lenore help a peasant fighter to his feet, putting a sword back in his hand. He saw Odd move back, sword held ready.

Greave braced himself for the next strike of Ravin's forces... and that was when he saw the reinforcements starting to come from the city.

They didn't look like southerners. Instead, they looked like noble retainers, led out from the eastern gate of the city. There weren't many of them, though, certainly not as many as Greave had feared. None at all came out of Royalsport from the west. The numbers were not the devastating tide they could have been, and Greave found himself grateful for that.

When Renard had told them that the House of Sighs was working to draw away Ravin's allies, Greave had wondered how effective their approach could be. Now he could see exactly how much they'd been able to do in the empty spaces where there could have been men trying to encircle his sister's forces.

He could see what Ravin's plan had been now. He'd been trying to get Lenore to commit to her strike, to wear her down, and then to enclose her forces in a circle of steel so that they couldn't get away while he crushed them. Instead, that circle would be incomplete now, leaving fewer foes to fight, and a path to escape if they failed.

Greave swallowed at the thought of that. That was the problem with Ravin's plans. He was clever enough to move himself into a position of strength before he acted, so that even once his plans were known, it was hard to do anything about them.

Had he calculated everything correctly? Against such a powerful enemy, there were no certainties. The best plan in the world could still fail, if luck went against them, or their foes just proved too strong.

"Why are they waiting?" Erin asked.

"They want us to see that we've lost," Greave said. "They want us to see that they're more powerful, and we can't win."

He had to remind himself that there were other reasons too. It was easy to forget that Ravin's army would be tired and hurt too. They'd suffered losses, and the men would be just as exhausted from the pushing and shoving of the battle lines. It was easy to forget that their foes were human, as prone to fear, pain, and exhaustion as anyone on their side was.

This was the time for a push. This was the moment when things could be won or lost. It was important to remember that they were not invincible. They *could* be beaten. At least, Greave had to hope that they could.

It was hard to feel certain of that, though, as Ravin's army rumbled forward again, moving into a charge aimed at the heart of Lenore's forces. Those horsemen who hadn't lost their mounts gave bloodthirsty cries as they galloped forward. Heavily armored men locked their shields as they attacked in a wall. Skirmishers threw short axes or drew daggers. Where before, Lenore's forces had struck at Ravin's in a wave, now it was his on the attack.

This army wasn't a wave. It was an iron fist punching into the heart of Lenore's forces. At the start of the battle, that might have allowed the strong forces on the flanks to fold in and crush the attackers, but now her lines didn't have that power left. Greave heard the impact of the charge even as far away as he was, the screams and the violence renewing themselves in one horrible clash.

Greave saw men cut down in that first clash, saw bodies broken, saw people just trampled. The air was thick with screams and the scent of death, and it seemed that every second he waited now was one in which more people died, and more still.

He looked over at Erin's face and he could see the fear there as she watched the battle. It wouldn't be fear for herself, because Erin was the least afraid person he knew, but he could see her horror at the number of men who were dying, and her worry for Lenore as the combined forces of Ravin's army tried to batter their way through to her.

"Greave," Erin said. "We have to *do* something."

Greave nodded. At this point, there was no more waiting. There was no more standing by, just watching everyone die. Greave just hoped that he hadn't left it all too late. He told himself that they'd had to wait, had to see what Ravin was going to do, but now it seemed like Lenore's forces were about to be overrun, and all their planning was going to be for nothing.

In that moment, Greave knew that he had no more choices. Planning had made the whole battle seem simple and obvious, every step of it set out one after another. Yet now, with enemies closing in on every side, there *were* no more choices. The only thing to their advantage was that the lack of foes on one side at least left them with a way to run.

Greave took out a hunting horn, high pitched but still able to sound over the field. He took a deep breath, holding it to his lips. Then he blew a series of blasts into it, sounding the retreat.

CHAPTER TWENTY SIX

F or what seemed like the hundredth time, Devin looked over the castle, trying to find a way in. His hand closed in frustration over the
grip of the sword he'd made as he looked at the solidly closed gates, the
high walls, the guards pacing atop them.

He looked past all that, to the spot where the sorcerer's tower sat alongside the keep. Devin thought he'd seen movement there, but he couldn't
tell whether it was Master Grey, Anders, or someone else entirely.

Sigil whined, coming out from the shadows and looking toward the
gates. He was obviously as eager to act as Devin was, but there seemed
to be no way in, no matter how hard he looked.

Devin put his hand against Sigil's fur, deepening his connection to
the magic around him, letting him see the world more clearly, and the elements that connected it together. He found himself half hoping that there
would be a secret way for sorcerers, only visible through their sight, or
that the insight that came with the magic would make it easy to see how
to open up a gate in the castle walls. Sadly, he just found himself staring
at the stones in frustration.

He'd thought that getting the sword would be the hard part of this,
yet in a lot of ways, this had proved to be the easiest component. It had
taken one lie to part Finnal from the sword, yet Devin knew that it would
take far more than that to get him inside walls that were sealed off tight.

Devin considered the problems. The gates were closed, and weren't
likely to open for the likes of him when there was a battle on. There were
still men there in front of them, apparently from the retinues of Finnal
and others, although many more seemed to have spread out, off about
tasks of their lords' choosing. The walls were high and largely smooth

sided, while the guards atop them were armed with bows that could probably pick off anyone who came too close, too openly.

He had some advantages, of course. He had the sword, and in any fight, a blade made from star metal would be a major advantage. He had Sigil to lend him an advantage in connecting to the magic around him. He had all the magic that he'd learned to do so far, although if there was one thing he'd learned, it was that magic *wasn't* something one simply learned and then did at will. Each situation had new variables to balance, so that being able to do something once didn't guarantee being able to do it again.

The trouble was, while all of those advantages might have been useful in a fight, that was the last thing Devin needed right then. He needed to find a way to get into the castle quietly. He crouched in the shadows, trying to consider his options.

He couldn't just demand entry. Even the best lie probably wouldn't work on soldiers determined to keep everyone out. Devin could try fighting his way in, but with so many men there, even a sword as fine as the one he'd made wouldn't help enough. Even if he somehow cut through them, the gates would still be shut, and by then, men would be raining arrows down on him.

Maybe there was some magic that could blast the gates open, or just force them to unlock elegantly at his approach. The trouble was that Devin didn't know for sure, and he wasn't likely to discover that magic in the middle of a fight. Even if he *did* somehow open the gate like that, the effort of it would probably drain him, while simultaneously alerting Anders to his presence.

The direct approach seemed to be out. What did that leave? Climbing the walls? He couldn't hope to do that in daylight, and even if he had dark on his side, there was too much that might go wrong. Whatever he tried, there was still the problem of the few guards left within being able to see Devin as he approached, and what they might do once they decided that he was a threat.

"Come on, think," he whispered to himself. If there was one thing he'd learned so far out in the world, it was that being a sorcerer was less about doing amazing feats of magic on a whim and more about careful thought mixed with perfect preparation. Yet there wasn't any obvious path here, wasn't any clue as to where to begin.

Devin set off into the streets, working around the castle, hoping to see more. And he did, but not at all in the way he'd expected. What he saw was a group of people in clothes that weren't at all fine enough for the noble quarter, moving through the streets, armed with hammers and knives, axes and clubs. There were around a dozen of them, moving furtively.

Devin almost avoided them on instinct, but then he considered one last part of Master Grey's art: the idea of things fitting together, of being in the perfect place for the events of destiny to take their course. Certainly, part of it seemed to be spotting the shifts in circumstances, and finding ways to turn them into things that moved toward his goals. What if this *was* Devin's chance?

He knew he couldn't risk just standing there, not when he had so few other options, so he moved out into the street to intercept the group. They stopped short, although Devin suspected that had more to do with Sigil's presence than with his. Several of them backed away from the wolf, although a few more raised their weapons, as if they might attack.

"Who are you?" a woman with them demanded. "Are you with the uprising, or the invaders?"

That was a dangerous question to answer, since Devin had no idea if these people were there trying to fight against Ravin's control of the city, or if they were Quiet Men in disguise, trying to root out traitors.

A man stepped forward. "It's all right, Bethe. I know who he is."

Devin stared at him, trying to picture where he'd seen him before. He tried to look past the rough peasant clothing, the mud, the scrapes and the bruises. He found himself imagining the figure before him in richer clothing, standing over him ready to kill him for the crime of raising a hand to him.

"You're—"

He saw Vars raise a hand, and Devin stopped short.

"I know who I was," he said. "And I know who *you* are. The boy who made a sword at the sorcerer's behest."

"Two swords," Devin said. He touched the one he'd made for the wedding. "I have one here."

It wasn't quite a threat, but the truth was that Devin didn't like Vars, and he certainly had no reason to see him as a friend. He didn't know the people with the prince, but it stood to reason that a man like Vars would attract thieves and ruffians more readily than he would honest folk. Several of them didn't look happy at Devin's presence.

"Devin," Vars said, "I need you to put aside what you know about me, or think you know about me. What are you doing out here, so close to the castle?"

"Trying to get inside," Devin admitted. He didn't want to risk telling Vars too much. "There are … things I need to do in Master Grey's tower."

"Things that might be important in all the ways only sorcerers know about?" Vars said. Once, there might have been contempt dripping from his voice. Now there only seemed to be a kind of weariness at the way the world worked.

"There may be someone there who has a sword that can stop a dragon," Devin said. "A sword I made, and he stole."

"And you're going to get it back?" Vars said. He looked around. "*We're* going to take back the castle."

"Just the dozen of you?" Devin asked.

"More, and they would see us coming," the woman with Vars, Bethe, said. She sounded determined as she hefted a club that looked far too much like a rolling pin.

"And why are you doing that?" Devin asked. This was the problem. The very fact that Vars was here suggested that he should be trying to stop this, even though it sounded like they were trying to get to the same place.

The woman paused, looking from Devin to Vars and back. "You know him, don't you?" she said to Devin. "You know … who he was?"

Devin nodded.

"He's not that man anymore," Bethe said. "Or maybe he is, but he's trying to do the right thing. He saved my life, and this … the idea is that we take the castle to stop Ravin getting it back."

She sounded sincere, but that didn't necessarily mean anything when it came to Prince Vars's motivations. Trusting him would be like asking a snake not to bite. Yet what other choice did Devin have right then?

"Ravin treated me like nothing," Vars said, lowering his voice and moving closer. "He hurt me, and his men tried to do more to Bethe. I don't care about much, but I care about *her*. I'm *going* to do this, with or without your help."

"How were you even planning to get into the castle?" Devin asked.

"I know a way," Vars insisted. "The same way that I got out when I ran. There's a tunnel."

"And you think Ravin won't have something like that guarded?" Devin asked. "You think he won't have had it walled off after you left, or laced it with traps?"

"Then it's a good thing that I have a sorcerer's apprentice to help me get through those things," Vars replied, a trace of the old sharpness there in his voice. "We need one another. Neither of us will get into the castle without the other. What you do after that is up to you."

Devin considered it. This wasn't even about trust at this point, just need. He needed Vars to get in there. After that, well, the prince and his companions would be on their own.

Chapter Twenty Seven

Ravin should have been savoring his triumph. Instead, he felt his blood boiling in anger, even as he killed foe after foe. Where were his noble reinforcements? Where were the ones who had sworn to obey their new emperor in all things?

He knew where they were, even as he hacked his sword through the shoulder of a man who was backing away, raising his hands as if that might stop Ravin from killing him. They were waiting to see what would happen. *That* thought made him strike a second blow at his already falling foe, sending blood spraying out over Ravin.

What was one more spray of it when he was already covered in blood? How many enemies had he cut down now? How many of his own men had fallen around him, killed in the chaos of the battle? Enough that his gilded armor was stained as red as the clothes he wore beneath. Enough that his blade was stained with it now.

When this was done, he would stain it again with the blood of those who had betrayed him. Did they think he didn't know what they were doing? Did they think that they could just sit back until the final moments of the battle and then come in, trying to look loyal to whoever won?

No, Finnal and his father had shown their true colors now. They were men who bent in the wind like reeds, hoping for their own advantage. They were men who were probably plotting, even now, how to wrest his kingdom from him. Ravin would see them impaled in front of their retainers, and would then see those retainers dead. He roared and struck out at the next of the foes before him, and the next.

The few who had come in from the eastern gate would be permitted to live, and would even advance thanks to their loyalty, but Ravin's fury was too great to feel grateful for that. An emperor shouldn't feel *happy* that his commands were being obeyed by the dogs who served him. He should simply expect it, and it should happen.

In any case, he didn't *need* allies right now, just the force and fury that had propelled him into the position he possessed. For all that his rule involved cunning and control, at the heart of it there had been the ability to inspire men to follow him, and the ability to lead in the heart of the fight. He did it now, battering aside a sword blow, kicking a man out of his path. He led his men deep into the heart of Lenore's forces, and now there was no grand strategy to it, no careful maneuvering for advantage. There was only the impact of the charge and the thrill of violence all around him. A great leader seized moments like this, knowing when to utterly destroy his enemies.

Before him, they were starting to take steps backwards under the weight of the assault, giving ground in a way that made it clear that Ravin didn't *need* the support of his so-called allies in order to win this.

He heard the moment when the horn blasts came, from over behind their lines. For a second, Ravin wondered about what it might mean, then the forces before him *showed* him what it meant, backing away, then turning and running.

Ravin cut down the ones who were the first to turn, their exposed backs providing a target that was too tempting to ignore. He sliced across one of them, plunged his blade into another, and laughed, loud enough that the men around him would all be able to hear.

"Look at them, the cowards!" he bellowed. "They thought they could defeat me, but they have failed, like all the ones before!"

He saw Lenore among the ones fleeing. Had she been the one to order the retreat, or had she had another watching, making those decisions? It didn't matter; what mattered was that she was fleeing, the men around her fighting their retreat, her terror as she ran palpable. Her muddied, bloodstained dress trailed behind her like a pennant as she ran, and Ravin laughed again at the sight of her like that.

They probably thought that they could get away, now that they weren't fully encircled thanks to the absence of his allies. They couldn't. Ravin would chase them down if it meant hunting them to the ends of the

Northern Kingdom. He would stain this field with their blood and put an end to the petty rebellion once and for all.

He pointed. "After them, kill them all. All except Lenore. Gold to the man who brings me the princess, alive!"

That got a roar of approval from his men. The great mass of them started forward, men from a dozen different parts of his empire turned into one avenging fist of iron and death. With the thunder of booted feet on churned up ground, they set off in pursuit of their vanquished foes.

⚜ ⚜ ⚜

Greave had to struggle to keep fear from consuming him as he saw Lenore's forces start to retreat. Before all of this started, he'd been so certain about his planning, yet now, as his sister's soldiers fell back, Greave could only see the ones being cut down from behind, the ones who would never see their families again.

Were their deaths his fault? Should he have sounded the withdrawal earlier, before Ravin's forces charged? Should he not have sounded it at all? His fears ran through him, mingling with guilt as he stared out at the dying.

The biggest fear would be that Ravin's forces would simply run those of his sister down and slaughter them as they ran, turning the retreat into a rout, and then a massacre. If he'd misjudged this retreat, they wouldn't have enough space to run, wouldn't make it back to the line of half-built siege gear that served as a rough barricade across the field they were in, wouldn't even get close to the dark and welcoming embrace of the forest beyond.

"Now?" Erin asked, beside him. She was bouncing lightly on her toes in spite of the bandages that poked out from beneath her armor, hinting at the wounds beneath. She looked eager, almost... feral.

Greave shook his head. "We have to hold here. We have to wait for them."

"Lenore is in danger, Greave," Erin said. "I'll not stand here."

"You will," Greave said. "We have to."

To him, Erin looked as if she might charge down in spite of everything they had discussed, everything that they knew needed to happen. "Do you think I don't *want* to help?"

Erin looked over at him, and she paused. "Greave... look at it all."

Greave was already watching. He could see all kinds of figures running out across the fields, his sister at their head so that the rest of her army seemed like the tail of a comet behind her. He saw men and women running for safety, trying to outpace their opponents when they knew that they couldn't fight them head on.

He saw Odd making a fighting withdrawal, turning seemingly at random as he ran to cut down this or that foe. He spun even as Greave watched, sword lancing out to claim a victim, before he helped another soldier to his feet. It was something Greave had never thought to see from a man who had been the mad knight.

"Now?" Erin asked, more urgently this time.

Still, Greave shook his head. It hurt to do it, hurt to have to watch the dying, but he'd given his sister his word. They would wait here.

"No," he said.

"Greave!"

Below, those closest to the pursuing forces were dying. In a retreat like this, skill at arms didn't count for anything anymore. Greave thought he saw Lord Renslipp go down, hacked down from behind and then trampled on while his troops didn't even slow. What the old man was doing at the heart of the battle was anyone's guess, but Greave felt the loss of his bravery.

Archers shot arrows and crossbow bolts into the backs of the retreating forces, bringing people down indiscriminately. Since they were facing away to run they couldn't even use their shields to protect themselves, and Greave saw an armored knight brought down with a dozen bolts in his back.

The screams were the worst part of it, the dying screams of the fallen mixed with cries of pain from the wounded and cries of terror from those who were running for their lives. The whole mingled together, twisted by the sounds of hate coming from the pursuing army of King Ravin, turned into a cacophony that was painful for Greave to hear.

"Now?" Erin asked, and she looked as if she might burst if Greave didn't say yes.

"Almost," he replied. "A few more paces. A few more."

"How *many* more?" Erin demanded, but Greave was already trying to decide that. How much further could he let this go on? How long could he hold back? He mentally drew a line on the ground, trying to gauge the speed of the retreat and the commitment of those chasing after them. It felt sickening, trying to engage in something so purely intellectual when people were dying in front of him, but he knew he had to do it. He had to get this right.

Lenore's people were running past him now, so that it seemed that he stood alone before the might of Ravin's forces bearing down on them. It was terrifying.

"Now?" Erin asked, yet again, and this time, Greave gave her what she wanted. He nodded.

"Now."

He lifted his horn to his lips, took another breath, and for the second time that day blew a series of notes upon it. He blew with all his might, terrified that the horn might not be enough to be heard above the sounds of the battle, blast after blast from it, determined to make this moment count.

For a second, there was nothing except the enemy army bearing down on the retreating forms of Lenore's soldiers. For a moment, Greave thought that he'd misjudged it, that he'd left it too late.

Then horns blared in answer, and the fields and the forest erupted with men.

CHAPTER TWENTY EIGHT

A round Erin, the ground seemed to surge as men and women rose up, throwing aside cloaks and rising in their lines, ready for the attack. Behind her in the trees, more surged forward, emerging from the tree line led by Lord Ness and Lord Welles.

The ones around Erin rose up in a wave, weapons already drawn, and Erin felt a moment of pride at it, because she'd helped to dig the pits in which they'd hidden in the dead of night, covering them with leaf – and grass-strewn cloaks so that Ravin wouldn't spot them.

At the same time, Lenore's forces turned, forming ranks in a way that shouldn't have been possible mid-rout, except that they'd practiced for exactly this. They knew that they had to hold out for the seconds it took for the others to reach them.

"Charge!" Erin yelled, and the others around her started forward at a full sprint. They were still fresh, still had the energy for the charge, and they were closing the distance between themselves and the enemy force before Ravin's forces could even begin to reform into coherent lines rather than one mob of chasing soldiers.

Erin ran, and in the seconds it took to close the distance, she couldn't help but think of her brother's military brilliance, grinning wildly at how expertly he'd tricked the most dangerous general of the age.

When Greave had explained his plan, Erin had thought that it was dangerous, and had the potential to get them all killed. Hide in the woods? Dig pits in the *fields*? Erin had wanted to know exactly what kind of general would think of doing that. Of course, Greave had been ready with a dozen historical examples.

Looking back, the reasoning had been simple. It had been obvious that Ravin would have a plan, obvious that he would try to trick them in some way. It was also obvious that he would expect *them* to try some trick, some strategy. That was why they'd brought along the unfinished line of siege engines, so that Ravin could puzzle them out as some kind of defensive fortification and think that he'd fathomed their plan.

After that, they'd robbed him of his allies using the House of Sighs. If he'd still had the full weight of the lords behind him, then it was likely that no plan could have overcome the difference in numbers.

Then, it was about his one weakness: he thought that those who opposed him were weak compared to him, that they could never truly match up to him.

Looked at like that, it made *sense* to lure him in, to send in only a portion of their army to wear him down and then retreat, luring him off the ground of his choosing and onto the ground they'd prepared. Even as Erin thought it, a squadron of horse archers trying to flank the newly charging force ran into the tripwires that Greave and a handful of others had set out on the edges of the field, horses screaming as they went down. Somewhere in his travels, her brother had gotten *sneaky*.

There was no time for more thought, though, because there was still a danger in this plan that made Erin's heart clench with the thought of it. There was only so far that Ravin's forces would follow a retreating force before they worked out that something was wrong, only so close they could be allowed to get to the hidden pits and the trees. That meant that for a few crucial seconds, Lenore's line still had to hold. Even when Erin's line hit them, there would still be more time before the ones from the trees got there. No city let trees get *too* close to the walls, for precisely this reason.

She saw Ravin's forces reel as Lenore's people turned, cutting into them. She saw men almost run onto the blades and the spears presented there, her sister raising her own sword high, calling out to the men.

"Now!" she called. "Cut them down before they reform!"

They struck out at their foes, stabbing out from a solid line of shields and armor. Erin pushed forward, ignoring the pain in her side from her battered ribs and the wounds that had needed to be stitched. She'd fitted a new haft to her spear herself, and she held it at shoulder level as she ran, as if she might throw it, with a buckler strapped to her left arm.

She *did* throw it as she hit the battle line, hard enough that it plunged into the throat of a large, bearded brute in front of her. She batted aside a sword blow with her buckler, ducked under the sweep of another blade, and snatched the spear back up even as the rest of her troops hit the enemy line.

It wasn't like a wave breaking on the shore now. Instead, it was like the tip of her spear, plunging deep into its target. Ravin's men were still trying to gather themselves, trying to make sense of what was happening, and every second that they spent trying to do it was a second in which more of them died.

Erin killed her share and more. She couldn't dance through the battle the way she might have without her wounds, the way Odd had taught her to, but she still had the skills she'd built up with the Knights of the Spur. She deflected blows and thrust with her spear, cut across throats and hamstrings with the broad blade of it and used her new buckler to make up for the restricted movement because of her side.

A man came at her, swinging a flail. Erin reached up to parry it and the flail wrapped around it, the man yanking her in toward him. Erin went with the move, riding the momentum of it and driving her spear deep into his chest. She let go of her spear for a moment as she heard another man coming at her back, deflecting the stroke of a sword and moving in, drawing a dagger and stabbing again and again.

She recovered her spear and looked around for more foes. She saw Lenore and Greave fighting close to one another, and that was probably the right thing, because it meant that the strongest troops could protect both of her siblings more effectively.

Erin didn't *want* to be protected. She'd hated being left behind from the main assault, hated not being able to protect her sister in that first phase. She hadn't wanted to stand by when Lenore could have been cut down at any moment in that attack. She'd understood that her sister had needed to be out there in front to draw Ravin's attention, but she'd wanted to be there too in order to protect her.

There was another reason too, one that pushed Erin forward, making her cut her spear blade across the stomach of one man, thrust the point up through another man's skull. Ahead, across the battlefield, she could see

Odd fighting, breathtaking in the smoothness and the speed of his attack, silence and fury seeming to blend now in something that was far beyond anything Erin had seen of him in practice. She saw him step in toward the stroke of a sword and somehow he wasn't there anymore, changing the angle just slightly and taking his opponent's head from his shoulders in one smooth movement.

He moved again, and more men died. Erin started to fight her way toward him, all the while wondering how much he had been holding back when they'd trained. This was something close to perfection, an art that probably only a few people in the kingdom had enough skill to appreciate. Erin was so entranced by it that she barely slipped aside from an axe blow in time, her side in agony with the effort of the movement. She thrust her spear into her attacker's heart, but for a moment she fell to one knee, the pain too great to keep going.

Maybe she should have stayed back where she was, behind the lines. Uninjured, she would have backed herself to fight almost any man in the kingdom, but here, like this...

Anger flashed through Erin. No, she *would* keep going. She wouldn't let her pain stop her. Some things couldn't be forgotten, no matter how much others might want her to, and how dangerous the foe to come was. She pushed back to her feet, using the movement to drive another spear blow into a foe, and plunged on through the battle in the direction of her enemy.

Anything could happen in a battle: a spear blow could come out of nowhere, death could come without warning. She might have told her sister that she'd learned her lesson, might have made it seem that she'd put aside her hatred, but this would be the moment when she settled things.

She saw him then, standing at the heart of the fighting, swinging his sword with a grace and rage that seemed at odds with everything else. Ravin was there, his armor red with blood, a pile of foes at his feet.

Erin started to cut her way through the foes who stood between them. She sidestepped a thrust and cut her spear into a man's throat. She cried out in agony as a mace hit her side, but retaliated by cutting the man's legs from under him. An arrow grazed her cheek, and Erin tasted blood, but it missed her barely, going on to strike someone behind her in the chest.

She saw Ravin cutting down another man then, fighting his way forward, heading for Lenore. She plunged forward, determined to kill him before he could get to her sister, but that was when the third wave of troops slammed into the fight, pressing the melee tighter, throwing her against a foe so that there was fresh agony in her ribs. She fell, and it took all her effort to get back to her feet.

She looked around, but couldn't find Ravin now. With a scream of frustration, Erin threw herself forward, determined to find him again.

CHAPTER TWENTY NINE

Renard had never been entirely at home in large, angry crowds, possibly because it was often him they were angry with. Now though, he stood exultantly on Royalsport's streets as people poured out onto them, ordinary people, people from all walks of life.

There were people from the poorest districts, dressed in ragged clothes. There were people who came out dressed as if this were another day of business at the House of Merchants, rather than an uprising. There were even one or two who were more richly dressed than that, looking around nervously as if unsure that they really belonged there.

They'd armed themselves with whatever they could find, but Renard knew from experience that a kitchen knife could be as dangerous as a sword at close quarters. Their seemingly ever-growing force started to wash through the streets, picking up people as it went, like the streams that washed between the islands of the city being fed by tributaries.

The first group of guards they ran into found themselves swept away by that flow, their armor and their weapons counting for little when there were so many people involved. Renard lunged at one of the guards, knocking aside his attempt to stab another of those out there and bringing an elbow around sharply into the man's jaw, clubbing him into unconsciousness. The other guards there weren't so lucky, stabbed by a variety of homemade weapons.

"For the queen!" The cry seemed to go up spontaneously, but Renard had enough experience with Meredith's people to look around the crowd, spotting the people who were starting the cry. He was pretty sure he remembered seeing some of them at the House of Sighs.

He certainly knew *one* of them. Meredith was there, people running to her and then away, no doubt carrying instructions designed to shape the progress of the crowds through the streets.

"I didn't think you would come out here with the rest of us," Renard said. When she'd said that it was time for the House of Sighs to act, Renard had pictured her sitting there like a spider at the heart of her web while others took on the dangerous tasks out in the streets.

He had the sense not to say *that* part to her, at least.

"Where else did you think I would be?" Meredith countered. Renard noted that she'd changed her dress to something simpler, obviously designed to fit in with the ordinary people while still managing to stand out. He couldn't see any weapons on her, but he had no doubt that they were there.

"What now, then?" Renard asked.

"Ravin's full forces are at the southern gates," Meredith said. "So we will take people out of the eastern and western ones. I will lead the force to the east."

"And who leads the one to the west?" Renard asked.

Meredith made a face. "Apparently, an idiot who doesn't even know when he's being given an important responsibility."

"What?" Shock hit Renard. "Me?"

"Of course you," she said. "Out the western gate, hit them in the flank. Go, I'll meet you in the middle."

The briskness with which she said it would have suited any general. She turned and set off, plenty of those there following her. Renard realized that he would have to make an effort, or it would just be him on his own trying to take the western gate.

"Follow me!" he called out. "To the western gate!"

Some did, especially when some of the others from the House of Sighs started to call out alongside him, making sure of it. Aurelle was there in the crowd, and she seemed more determined than the rest to make her way forward.

They flowed through the city en masse, and when they met small groups of guards, those guards ran or died. One group stood and tried to fight, a man lunging forward at Renard. He managed to block a blow using a long knife, stabbing the man with one held in his left hand and moving forward.

For a man who generally tried to avoid violence, he seemed to be moving toward a battle in far too much of a hurry.

They poured across one of the small bridges, and the best part about a force like this was that it only grew inside as it went along. Where other armies would have driven people back inside, afraid for their lives, this one seemed to suck up people as it went, so that soon, Renard found himself at the head of a horde of the common folk.

They made their way toward the western gates, and the guards on those gates simply ran in the face of the numbers of them. Renard pointed to a group of the people following him. He wasn't used to giving orders, but he could pretend that he was, at least for now.

"You, hold the gates. Make sure the guards don't come back," he said, hoping that they wouldn't ask basic questions like how, or why, or what to do if there were more guards than before. For the moment, at least, Renard's luck seemed to be holding.

Then they opened the gates, and he cursed himself for even *thinking* it.

A force of what were clearly a nobleman's retainers stood there in perfect lines, as if waiting for their moment to join the battle. Renard's heart all but stopped in his chest, as he realized that he was going to have to decide now if they should pull back or charge forward, trying to take on this waiting, fresh, well-equipped force of soldiers.

The two forces stood there facing one another, and Renard didn't know what to do. A cluster of what were obviously noblemen stood toward the front, and two of them, a younger man and an older one, seemed to be the ones in command.

They stood there, staring at Renard, or maybe it just felt like they were. Maybe they were just looking at the huge force of common folk around him, trying to work out what it meant for them, if *they* should attack, or pull back, or do something else. The tension of the moment dragged out, and dragged out.

Renard found himself laughing. It was inexplicable, sudden, and unstoppable.

"What are you laughing at?" Aurelle asked, from close by his side.

"They don't know," he managed, in between bursts of laughter. "They don't know what to do either."

She didn't look like she was in a mood for laughter. "That's Duke Viris and his son Finnal. The world would be a better place if we killed them both."

There was more hatred there in her voice than Renard had heard when she was talking about anything else. At the same time, Renard knew that just charging into such solidly held ranks would be suicide. They needed to find another way.

"Dying fighting them doesn't get you to Prince Greave," Renard said. It was a harsh move, but he knew he had to make it.

Aurelle gave him a hard look, and then nodded. "Wait here."

"Why?" Renard asked.

"Because as much as I like you, you have a knack for saying stupid things at the wrong moment. Wait *here*, Renard."

He did as she asked, and it was probably just as well, because if he'd started across the space between the two forces with her, he suspected that all the people there would have followed him. Then they would have been stuck in a battle by the gate, rather than getting to the battle they really wanted to be in.

Wanting to be in a battle? Renard couldn't help but marvel at the ways in which his life had changed. Some of them might have been for the better, but then again, he'd still spent most of the last few weeks running, hiding, being attacked, and more.

He stood there, watching Aurelle cross the space between them, wondering if he'd just made a mistake. What was to stop her from drawing a knife and cutting the throats of the men she hated so much? If she did that, then there would be a battle here, without a doubt. Renard could see the retainers lined up there, looking like they were ready to march forward at any moment. Behind *him,* the crowd of their army was pressing forward, so that it felt as if Renard was having to hold back their whole weight by himself.

He saw Aurelle reach Duke Viris and Finnal, and the fact that he couldn't hear any of what was going on there only made it worse for him.

Was she calling out threats to them as she walked up? Was she approaching with sweet words so that she could get close enough to stab them? He saw her offer them an elegant curtsey, but that didn't necessarily mean anything; it might just be a way for her to get close enough to attack them both.

The next few seconds were among the most tense of Renard's life. Aurelle was talking to the two of them, and Renard was too far away to really judge their reactions. He didn't know if they were going to have a battle or something else, and the not knowing was killing him.

Even when Aurelle turned and walked away, Renard didn't dare breathe a sigh of relief. She hadn't killed them, but that didn't mean anything. It didn't guarantee that Duke Viris and his son wouldn't order their troops forward. Even now, they looked as though they were on edge, ready to charge forward at any moment.

Then Finnal barked out an order, and the men there turned on their heels, marching away, withdrawing into the countryside.

Renard *did* breathe a sigh of relief, then, but he knew that this was only the start. He gestured the people with him forward, starting to lead them around the side of the city, to a point where he could see the battle ahead of him. They were behind Ravin's forces, and he could see the intensity of the violence there.

He knew there was no time for hesitation. Stop now, and the people behind him would start to back away, their eagerness for the fight fading. *He* would probably react the same way, because he had no love for anything like this. He knew he had to give the order quickly, before his courage faded.

He pointed, trying to look more confident than he felt.

"Charge!"

CHAPTER THIRTY

Devin followed close behind Vars as the prince led the way down the passage he'd used to escape. They lit the way with lanterns, and Devin kept his hand in Sigil's fur, concentrating on a different kind of sight.

Because of that, he saw the danger before the others. "Stop!" he called out. "Tripwires."

He knelt, looking at them. He didn't know what they were connected to, but the knowledge he'd gained from smithing let him at least guess at the way the mechanism worked. Cutting them wouldn't be enough; it would be better to pick their way between them.

"Step only where I step," he said.

He led the way, and Sigil seemed to sense the danger of the wires too, stepping over them carefully. The others followed, and Devin held his breath, hoping that each of them would make it through unscathed.

"Why haven't they done more to block this off?" Devin asked Vars.

The former prince shrugged. "The tunnel floods when the water's high enough. Maybe they didn't think it needed guarding. More to the point, how did *you* manage to spot the tripwires?"

The others were looking at him too, as if they couldn't quite understand how he'd managed it. Devin wasn't sure if he could explain that the first part of magic was looking at the world more closely, seeing it as it really was. He wasn't sure if explaining that would make them look at him with more awe, or less.

"I just saw the glint of them," he said instead, and they kept going down the tunnel.

It came out in a space near the castle courtyard, and for a moment, they were all blinking in the light. Devin recovered in time to see guards simply staring at them, not knowing what they were doing there.

He and the others reacted before they did, rushing forward with weapons drawn. A guard swung a sword at him and Devin met it with his star metal blade, knocking it aside and then cutting the man down in one smooth movement. He saw another guard sneaking up behind Vars and plunged the sword into the guard's ribs, deep enough that the tip emerged from the other side of his torso.

The fight around the entrance to the tunnel lasted only moments, but Devin knew that there would be more fights like it to come. Already, one of those who'd come through the tunnel was wounded, and he found himself wondering if they really had enough people to take on even the few guards Ravin would have left behind.

Devin knew that he couldn't go with them, though. Anders would be waiting for him in Master Grey's tower. Already, Devin could feel an energy coming from there that seemed to buzz on the edge of his consciousness. Whatever Anders was doing, it was powerful, and that meant that Devin needed to know what it was.

"Good luck with the rest of the guards," Devin said to Vars and the others.

"You're not staying until it's done?" Bethe asked him.

Devin shook his head, with a glance toward the tower. "I have my own business here, and from what I can feel, it can't wait."

Devin climbed the steps of Master Grey's tower, his eyes taking in the runes set on every surface, so that the tower became at once a conduit and a container of magical energy. He could see so much more now than he had before.

That was why, when he reached the first laboratory space of the tower, he could only stop and stare at the mess of it. It was as if someone had been searching for something, upending things until they found it. He reached out his senses, trying to understand it, and to his surprise found that the strange pulse of power that had drawn him here seemed to have stopped.

"I was wondering if you would come here first, or him," Anders said.

Devin looked around to see Anders descending the stairs from the living quarters above. He had Loss in his hand, unsheathed, the blade gleaming darkly. He looked a lot cleaner and harder edged than he had when he'd come to Devin's door, demanding the sword. His clothes looked new, richly patterned in dark velvet and silk. His eyes, meanwhile, seemed to hold nothing but contempt for Devin.

"I knew that eventually the sorcerer would come here," Anders said, standing on the last couple of stairs. "I should have guessed that he'd send his favorite first, though."

"Master Grey didn't send me," Devin said. "I came for the sword you stole."

Anders raised Loss almost casually. "It's in the hands it needs to be in, now. I'll say this much for you, Devin, you do make a very fine blade. It's a pity that's the extent of your talents."

"Give back what you stole, or you'll find out exactly what I can do," Devin said.

Anders laughed at that. "I saw your best back at that shack you call home. You're good while you have all the advantages, but now I'm the one with the sword you made." He nodded pointedly toward the stairs. "I let you live before. I think you're *trying* to be a good person, even if you've let yourself be used by the sorcerer, so I just stole the blade rather than cutting your throat. If you insist on fighting now though, I won't be so kind."

"I'm not helpless," Devin said. He drew his own sword, holding it two-handed and balanced in front of him.

"As you wish," Anders said, and he lifted his sword ready to fight. Devin lifted his own in a copy of the ready position he'd seen Swordmaster Wendros use back at the House of Weapons.

That was when Anders struck.

The first blow was lightning fast, and Devin saw the shock on the other boy's face as he parried it. Devin managed a smile.

"I made *two* swords out of star metal, not one," he said, and cut back at Anders furiously, in an exchange of blows that made the other young man give ground, heading back up the stairs.

Devin felt the moment when Anders pulled together magic, and moved aside from it just in time as a blast of force came past him, slamming into the stones of the tower, making them whine as the runes set there absorbed it.

Devin tried for a weaving of his own, seeing the way that Anders's feet were set on the stairs and trying to balance the forces necessary to stick his boots to the stone. For a moment, it seemed as if he had it, but then Anders kicked off backwards, jumping back upstairs so that Devin could only follow.

They fought their way through into a living space where the oddments that Master Grey had collected over the years had been placed in piles, presumably those Anders found useful and those he did not. Devin tried to keep the pressure on him, exchanging blows, giving him no time to formulate a strategy. Devin saw Sigil dart in toward Anders from the side, but Anders was quick enough to kick Sigil aside, making the wolf yelp.

Devin felt Anders try to piece together another fragment of magic, this one snagging at the edges of his mind, but Devin broke through it. As he'd found before when he was in contact with star metal, he could feel his connection to magic growing. He dared a web of spell strands designed to confuse and annoy, then lunged in behind them when Anders brushed them aside. He barely parried that lunge in time.

"Not bad," Anders said. He cut back at Devin. "But not enough, either."

His attacks came at Devin rapidly now, making Devin dance around the room to avoid them. Magically, Devin found that he had as much raw power as Anders, possibly more, but the other young man had more formal training, attacks flowing from him smoothly so that it was all Devin could do to shred them before they got too close to him.

Physically, it was almost the same story. Devin had a little more skill with the blade, but honestly, it was mostly things he'd picked up for himself, while Anders was all trained precision and expertly judged combinations of attacks.

If it had been just one or the other, Devin might have been able to cope. Even as it was, he tried a few cuts, wove together strands of magic, but Anders seemed to be able to deflect them each time. Yet, when it was swordplay and magic combined, the concentration needed to maintain them both was just too great.

Devin only faltered for a moment, but that was the moment in which Anders struck. Devin thought he saw an opening, but Anders caught his blade on Loss, and then kicked Devin back, hard, with a booted foot.

Too late, Devin realized that Anders had maneuvered him in front of the spiral stairs descending the tower. Too late, Devin tried to catch his balance, only to find his foot flailing at air. Another cut came at his head, and Devin realized that if he tried to keep his balance, that cut would land, decapitating him.

That left Devin with only one option: he let himself fall backwards.

He tumbled down the stairs, the edges of them slamming into his ribs, his back, his thighs as he turned over and over. The sword jarred from his hand, clattering down into the space below. It was probably just as well that Devin let go of it, because in the cascading tumble of it all, there would have been no way to keep from cutting himself.

He bounced from stair to stair, trying to cover his head with his arms to protect it. Despite that, something crashed against it, and Devin tasted blood.

He crashed to a halt, the world stopping its spinning around him. Devin, bruised and battered, was barely able to move. Above him, he could see Anders descending the stairs, Loss clutched in his hand, ready to finish him.

CHAPTER THIRTY ONE

Fury flooded through Ravin at the sight of a rabble converging on his forces from the rear, and at the sudden way Lenore's forces had turned about, striking at his army with all the skill and violence of real soldiers. He blocked the blow of a war hammer, cutting down the man who wielded it, and roared that anger.

"We will not lose!" he bellowed to his men. "Keep fighting, or I'll have your heads!"

The biggest part of his fury was that he had been tricked so successfully. Oh, people had tried to trick him in the past. They'd sent hidden assassins or tried betrayals, yet Ravin had always seen through those, as he had with Queen Aethe's uprising, or King Godwin's attempt to destroy the bridges. The ones who had tried to be direct, he had met with cunning, while the ones who had tried to be subtle he had met with overwhelming force.

Now, someone had outthought him, and worse, fresh troops were piling into his army from all sides. For the first time in a long time, he could feel his men giving ground against his orders.

Ravin cursed, and cut his way through to an open space. A pitchfork-wielding peasant stabbed at him, but Ravin hacked the weapon in half, and then them. A swordsman's cut found itself answered with a bind that left Ravin close enough to batter the man with one gauntlet-clad fist until he heard bone crunch and the man fell.

Briefly, a circle of his men gave Ravin time in which to think. Perhaps they were as sure as he was that no enemy could ever truly outthink him, or outfight him. Some of them, after all, had seen him conquer the deserts and would-be city states of the south, the individual principalities and the governorships. They had seen him win against cunning wood folk and stealthy, night-stalking killers. They believed in him, and in his destiny to unite the Three Kingdoms once more.

He would not fail them.

Ravin looked around, seeking inspiration or a way to make this right. For a moment, all he saw was the violence. He saw one of his men pinned down by two peasants while a third hacked at him with an axe, saw a bloodied knight exchanging blows with one of his Quiet Men and winning easily. None of it was what he wanted.

Then he saw her, as he had seen her before, standing at the heart of the violence. Lenore stood there with her sword raised as if it were a banner rather than a weapon, a symbol around whom her troops rallied, protected by men who Ravin could now clearly see weren't just peasants. The solution was simple.

"Men, form up on me!" he bellowed. "This is not done! This is a rabble, held together by the presence of their so-called queen. If we kill her, they will break, and they will flee!"

The strongest men he had formed a wedge around Ravin, with him at its heart. They were big men, well-armed and armored, carrying everything from great axes to lightning-fast curved swords. They had a determination to them now that Ravin had given his orders, but also a kind of relief. Their emperor had spoken, and now they knew how the world would be.

"Forward!" he commanded, and his wedge of men plunged back into the fray, making for Lenore.

They made the first few paces of progress quickly, because these *were* the strongest men of Ravin's army, and their foes mostly remained peasants and bandits, whatever banner they fought under now. For those few moments, Ravin didn't even have to kill anyone, because the blades around him did the killing for him.

It wasn't a sensation he enjoyed, and Ravin found himself almost grateful when men started to slip through the cracks of the formation, coming at him. He sliced the throat of a big, bearded man with an axe, then sidestepped the swing of a boy wielding a maul, shoving him to one of his other men to finish off.

The important thing was not to stop their progress, not to get bogged down in the fight. Battles were fickle things, and the minds of men more fickle still. It only took a man to break and run for a whole army to follow. Ravin had to get to Lenore, had to finish this, before it could get that far.

It was a pity, in a lot of ways, Ravin thought as he severed another limb from a foe's body, took another impact on his armor and kept moving. His plan before had been to kill her last, to make her watch the destruction of her army and then kill her slowly. That would have been a far more satisfying way to kill a foe who had angered him like this.

That had been before, though. Now, the priority was to get this done. Ravin would *not* see his dreams of empire fall apart because of the actions of some spoiled little princess whose only worth before had been to be married off to the highest bidder.

The thought distracted him enough that another blow clattered from his armor, and Ravin lanced his sword through his foe's chest, dragged it out, and lifted him, throwing him bodily into the melee before him in order to clear a space to move into.

His men started to die around him. The axe man at the point of the wedge fell with a sword sticking from his armpit, almost crushing the man who had killed him as he toppled. A swordsman found himself knifed by a peasant while he crossed blades with another opponent. Ravin cut both down in vengeance, but kept moving.

It didn't *matter* if his men died, didn't matter if they found themselves caught up in fights and peeled off from the wedge; all that mattered was that they kept making progress toward the princess before them. Ravin didn't even care if he killed the foes in front of him now, just so long as he hit them hard enough to move them from his path.

Men continued to fall around him, a skirmisher hacked down by an axe, a desert tribesman brought down by a spear. A more sentimental man might have seen the individual components of his hard-won kingdom being pulled from him one by one, but Ravin had never been that.

He thought of all the people he'd killed over the years, too many to count, even if he stuck to just those he'd ended with his own hands. They said that in battle most people just pushed and shoved, or struck blindly, hoping that someone else would do the real killing. Ravin had always been one of those with the knack for death, killing his share, and more beyond.

Men, women, children, beasts... all had fallen to his blade. He'd killed in battle and in intrigue, in executions and for simple sport, hunting those who had displeased him too greatly. Each death had been like a nail holding the great edifice of his kingdom together, from the first ones where he'd cleared away any of his father's seed who might prove a threat, to the great battles that had given him the throne.

Now, none of that mattered; only one death counted. If he could kill Lenore, then this was done. If not... no, there *was* no "if not." He was Ravin, and his destiny was too great to fail.

He was alone now, cutting his way through the battle, his two-handed sword cutting like a farmer's scythe, sweeping away enemies from his path. The fury and the certainty within him fueled him, letting him move forward with power and destruction. He cut the legs from under a foe, took the head from another. None of them had the talents to stretch his skills, but here in a battle that wasn't the test. The test that mattered was moving with efficiency, killing quickly without turning it into a fight, then moving on to the next foe.

Lenore was a few paces ahead now, hidden behind her wall of steel-clad men. Ravin charged forward then, smashing his shoulder into one of them, knocking him back. Another came at him, swinging a sword.

This foe was better than some of those Ravin had fought. His strikes were quick and deceptive, a feint coming in from the left before a blow swung at him from the right. Ravin read the stroke and parried it. He cut back, testing the other man's skills, and felt instantly where the weakness in him was. Ravin cut high, let his foe parry the stroke with jarring force, and then kicked out hard into the side of his knee.

As his knee buckled, Ravin changed the angle and cut through his neck, ending him. Ravin was already stepping over him as he died. This man didn't matter. The only thing that mattered was getting to Lenore, ending her, *winning* this.

She was there, ahead of him, just a few paces away now. Ravin took a step forward, and for a moment, the way to Lenore seemed clear, everyone around him engaged in fighting so many other people that they had no way to stop him. Ravin could already almost feel the moment when his blade would plunge home into Lenore's heart, the anticipation building in him until it was almost too great to bear.

He gave in to it, raised his sword, gave a roar, and charged forward to strike the blow that would secure his empire for him forever. He thought he saw Lenore start to turn toward him, perhaps alerted by his battle cry, but that didn't matter to Ravin. It only made things better, knowing that she would see the moment of her death coming, and that the sword she didn't know how to use wouldn't do *anything* to stop it.

Then something, some*one*, slammed into Ravin from the side, hitting him with their full weight and sending them both sprawling. Ravin rolled to his feet, and there, in front of him, stood Lenore's knight in monk's robes.

CHAPTER THIRTY TWO

The moment Odd saw Lenore in danger, it had cut through his battle rage like a knife. He flung himself through the battle without thinking about it, ducking under blades and dodging past spear heads. By the time he got close, Ravin was already into his killing blow, and there was only one thing that might stop it, so Odd flung himself at the emperor, slamming into him and tumbling with him to the ground.

Odd rolled to his feet smoothly, and wasn't surprised when Ravin came up just as quickly, his sword balanced in his hands, even as men started to pull Lenore away.

"Sir Oderick the Mad," Ravin said. "Come, show me that battle rage you're so famed for."

Odd smiled tightly. "With pleasure."

He came at Ravin fast, stopped his lunging stroke halfway, and changed direction to avoid Ravin's counterstrike. His own sword snaked out in the gap that Ravin had left, but the emperor was already moving away, taking the blow on a shoulder guard without injury. Odd saw his eyes widen slightly at that.

"You're good. Like the girl who tried to kill me. Shall I tell you how much I hurt her?"

Odd was attacking halfway through that, a clatter of strokes testing Ravin's defenses. Ravin stepped back, dragging one of his own soldiers into Odd's path so that the stroke sank into him rather than into the emperor. Ravin struck back, and Odd had to let go of his grip on his sword to avoid the attack, rolling and snatching up an arming sword one-handed from where it lay beyond the outstretched hand of a corpse.

Ravin was already coming at him again, so that Odd had to give ground, deflecting strokes with his newly claimed blade. Ravin slammed his shoulder into Odd, battering him back, but Odd responded by kicking out into the emperor's stomach, so that they both reeled from the impact.

Odd took the moment to snatch up a long knife in his left hand, using it to deflect the next blow that Ravin sent his way, cutting back with the arming sword so that it opened a gash along the emperor's arm.

"Is that the best you have?" Ravin said. "Where is the rage that killed a thousand foes? Where is the rage that burned villages?"

Odd showed him that rage then, unleashing it even as he fell into the monk's meditation, the two together surging as he struck blow after blow at Ravin. The emperor was as fine a swordsman as Odd had ever met, though, and unlike most of the truly skilled sword masters Odd had met, he seemed to have an inner core of rage of his own, so that blows went back and forth between them with uncanny speed and power.

The battle around them seemed almost to stop for them, or perhaps it was just that Odd's focus had narrowed to the point where only Ravin existed. He cut blistering patterns with his blade, moving from high guard to hanging, low to extended and back again, cuts coming in between each one. Ravin's answering blows made Odd's arms ring with their power, but there was nothing brutish and stupid about them. They caught on his blade, but then sought to change the angle. They seemed to be everywhere at once.

Odd had drawn first blood, but Ravin soon cut him in return, a searing line along his shoulder, only crossed blades keeping it from being more. Odd returned with a shallow wound to Ravin's thigh, received a smashing elbow to the face as they closed.

"You should be on my side," Ravin snarled as they stood there. "You wear the robes of a monk, but do you think a man like you can ever know peace? After all you've done? Step aside, let me kill the girl, and I'll give you battles that will let you run red with blood."

Something in Odd pulsed with savage joy at the thought of that, even as he flung his dagger at Ravin to create the room to escape. The emperor batted aside the blade. Odd flung his sword too, and then snatched up his original longsword from the fallen back of the man he'd killed with it.

He'd killed so many. Images of the dead threatened to overwhelm him, either with guilt or with the darker impulses that still flowed through him. Odd had thought that he'd found a space between the old rage and the things the abbot had tried to teach him, a clear, shining path where every step of the battle was like a dance. Now though, he felt as if he were nothing, just a butcher who had killed too many people to ever be allowed to live.

Ravin struck at him in that moment, and Odd barely parried the blow the emperor sent his way. He *didn't* fully parry the next one, the pain of it across his chest agonizing. Odd cut back, and Ravin parried it easily. The emperor kicked him to his knees.

"Time to finish this," he said, as the images of his past came to Odd again. One more image came to him though: of Lenore stepping out to meet the emperor bravely, knowing that he might cut her down, but still doing it because she knew that it was what was right.

In that moment, clarity came to Odd again, and he surged forward, striking at his foe. His first strike cut into Ravin's leg, deep enough to make him cry out. His second was partially parried, but he wound around the two-handed blade enough to pierce the tip of his longsword through a gap in Ravin's plate. Another burst of pain told him that Ravin had wounded him in response, but Odd didn't care.

There were those who said that battle was like a dance, but mostly that missed the point. Dancers didn't try to deceive one another with every movement, weren't trying to harm one another with every step. Yet in this space it *was* like that. Odd could see Ravin's movements with perfect clarity, and he was sure that the emperor was seeing him almost the same way, his rage lending him enough speed and strength that merely being able to see what was happening was not enough to react to all of it in time. Odd felt more cuts gather on his body, even as he inflicted them on his foe. Each one felt like a penance for one of the wrongs of his lifetime.

There had been a moment before, during the battle, when it had seemed that both his rage and the peace were building up inside him, working their way toward something more. Odd could feel the same sensation now, so that his sword sang with it, making music out of steel as it touched against Ravin's blade, forcing the emperor to set aside a sweeping blow aimed at his head, then leap a kick aiming to take his legs from under him.

A foe came in from the side and Odd killed him without even thinking, ducking then to avoid the emperor's blade. He tried a thrust at the emperor's stomach from low to the ground, rising like a boar's tusks, but all that did was to buy him space. Still the strange feeling was building inside Odd.

In that moment, it burst over him, in a wave of absolute peace, absolute knowing, so that just by looking at things around him, he understood them. Odd gasped with it, knowing that everything he'd thought he'd achieved before was a pale shadow of it. This, *this* was what the abbot had set him working toward, what they'd all been seeking, on Leveros.

Yet it *hadn't* been the abbot who had started all of this. Even as he parried another blow almost effortlessly, Odd could see every choice and consequence in his life laid out end to end. He could see how each one had affected everything that had come or would come. He saw the brutality of his past, saw the moment when he had locked away his blade tightly, determined to become a monk. He saw choice after choice, and now the decisions he saw were not his. He saw Ravin's choices reflected in everything he was, saw the lives and fates of every man and woman on the battlefield. His vision moved back, seeing the way that everything was connected, back before his birth, back before even the time of the dragons, cascading out from...

In that moment, the sheer scale of it was too much, but Odd still knew two things. The first was that he was not meant to be the one to kill Ravin, had *never* been meant to be the one to fulfill that role. *His* tasks in this had been many and varied, but they had not brought him to this point for that. They'd brought him here...

They'd brought him here for redemption.

That was the first thing Odd saw, and it was enough that tears filled his eyes at the thought of it, filled with joy, filled with hope. The second... the second was that he had already done all he needed to do in this place.

He looked round, knowing exactly which direction to look in. He saw Lenore there, being pulled away from Ravin's charge by her men, away from the one thing that might have changed this away from the direction it needed to go. All of this to bring him to this point, and he hadn't even needed to win the fight. He'd only needed to make it last long enough. Yet who else *but* him could have done that? This moment had *needed* a man poised between rage and clarity, skilled beyond almost any other with a blade, and so here he was.

The enormity of that was incredible to Odd, suffused with a sense of peace in a way he had never expected to feel in his life. He heard his blade clatter to the ground as he dropped it, and he turned to Ravin with a broad smile upon his face.

He was just in time for the emperor's two-handed sword to meet him, the point of it plunging through his heart. It hurt. How could it *not* hurt? And yet somehow, Odd kept smiling.

Even as he collapsed to his knees, he looked around the battlefield and saw Erin coming, a scream of rage and anguish upon her lips. He saw the figures closing in from every side.

"You've lost, monk," Ravin said as he drew his blade out. Odd collapsed to his back, with no more breath, no more strength. The darkness was closing in on him now.

Odd still smiled as he died though, because he knew. He knew that they had won, and so had he, in the only way that had ever really mattered. It was enough.

CHAPTER THIRTY THREE

E rin was already crying out in the moment when she saw Ravin's sword plunge into Odd's chest, but as he crumpled and died, she found herself silent, frozen. The whole battlefield seemed the same, but Erin didn't care then. She could only stare at the fallen form of Odd.

He'd meant so much to her, and she hadn't been able to truly tell him any of it. He'd been a mentor, a friend. She'd hated him for holding her back from killing, but she could see now that he'd just been trying to stop her from becoming what *he'd* been. It hurt to see him die at Ravin's hands like that, more than she could have even begun to imagine, and yet there had been one strange part about it... Odd had been *smiling* as the blade struck home.

Erin didn't understand that, couldn't understand that.

She also couldn't understand why things were suddenly so still and calm around her. She looked around, trying to make sense of what was happening, and that was when she saw the people there. They weren't Ravin's troops. They didn't even look like Lenore's troops, because even the least of those had some kind of armor or proper weapon. Instead, these looked like the ordinary people of the city, spread out around her, Ravin's forces overwhelmed and running as they came in numbers too great to deal with.

Erin saw people she recognized there: the thief Renard standing over the body of a foe with an almost embarrassed expression at having had to kill him, Lady Meredith of the House of Sighs standing there as if this were some jaunt into the country with a patron rather than a battle. *She* didn't seem bothered by the bodies at her feet in the least, Erin noted. As she continued to look around, she even saw her sister's former handmaid, Orianne. She saw Aurelle, the red-haired woman she'd met at the House of Sighs standing across from Greave, just staring at him as if she couldn't quite believe that he was there.

Around her, Ravin's men were mostly dead, or surrendering, or trying to run. Erin could see what had happened: not only had the House of Sighs managed to get rid of Ravin's allies, they'd brought a wave of people in to strike at his army from the rear. In the face of that, it had simply melted away.

Only not entirely. Some were starting to cluster around Ravin as if they might make some final, heroic stand against Lenore's entire army, and the whole city's worth of commoners that had joined them. Erin felt her blood boil at that. A man like that didn't deserve that kind of loyalty, didn't deserve to do *anything* that might be remembered. Yet there they were, trying to form up, trying to win this in spite of the situation.

"Men, to me!" she heard Ravin call. "To me!"

They came, surrounding him, some looking as if they were ready to die for their emperor, others looking as if they simply didn't know what to do next, other than this. They formed a wall of steel, ready to stand, and kill, and die.

And through it all, Lenore came forward, surrounded once more by her men, protected again from the danger that had almost claimed her just short moments ago. Odd had given his life to keep her from being cut down by Ravin, and another ruler might have taken that as a sign to step away and let her armies crush him. Not Lenore. She came forward with blood on her face and tears in her eyes, her dress torn away to reveal the armor beneath. Erin found herself both frightened by that and proud of her sister.

"You're standing with Ravin because you think everyone is the same as him," Lenore said, and her voice carried above the weird silence of the battlefield now. "You've seen the way he is after battles, willing to kill all who oppose him. You think that it's the only way to win wars, and so you think it's what I will do. You'd rather go down fighting."

Erin saw her sister start to walk toward them, throwing aside her sword and holding out her hands to them.

"It doesn't have to be that way," Lenore said. "You've been sold a dream of empire, and the strongest ruling, but there's a different way. There's peace. You *could* fight here, but you would lose, and you would die. You might kill a few more people before you died, but that would be the most you could achieve, and more death is nothing to take pride in."

She talked to them calmly, levelly, like a queen. She talked to them in a way that Erin never could have, and that she would never even have considered. She would have cut them all down without a second thought.

"Stop protecting a monster," Lenore said. "Join me instead. Live, rather than die."

In that moment, Erin saw her sister achieve more with a few words than she could have with a hundred spear thrusts. She saw the first few men edge away from Ravin, sheathing their weapons, looking almost surprised when the soldiers around them didn't instantly cut them down. They did it hesitantly, slowly, looking around for threats.

A few more joined them, and more after that, until all at once they joined the procession away from their leader, abandoning Ravin, leaving him standing over Odd's body in the middle of an empty space on the battlefield.

He stood there, surrounded now not just by an army, but by half the city. He stood there and somehow he still looked as if he had the authority of an emperor.

"I should have had you killed instead of kidnapped," Ravin said, as Lenore stepped into that space. There was blood on him from a dozen wounds, so that he seemed to lean on his great sword as much as hold it, barely able to stand.

"But you were like so many powerful men," Lenore said. "You thought of me as a prize to be taken, rather than as someone who could hurt you."

Ravin gave a choking cough, spitting blood. "So what now? Will you offer me the same terms as the fools who have abandoned me? Will you let me live if I pledge you my blade? Will you forgive me for cutting down your father, your mother, your brother, your friend?" He swept a hand toward Odd's fallen form, then made a mocking face. "Forgive me, oh great queen."

"Forgive you, no," Lenore said. "But I *will* allow you to leave this place, for the sake of peace. Walk from this battlefield, go back to your own kingdom, and never come back."

"You would offer me that?" Ravin said. "You know that for me to return a failure would almost guarantee my death? My subjects would rise up at such weakness."

"That is not my problem," Lenore said. "Be grateful that I am offering you even this much."

Erin couldn't believe what she was hearing. All of this, and her sister was going to let Ravin go? All the people he'd killed, all the chaos he'd caused, and she was going to let him just return to his own kingdom like nothing had happened? He was standing over Odd's body, smiling like a wolf, and Lenore was still moving closer, still trying to give him a way to end this peacefully?

In that moment, the feet that had been frozen to the ground with grief found a way to move again, and Erin started to push her way through the crowd.

"Of course, you will want guarantees," Ravin said. "Beneficial treaties and so on."

He was standing up straighter now.

"I don't care about any of that," Lenore said. Erin pushed past more people, shoving them aside, her feet building up to a run. Couldn't her sister see what Ravin was? Couldn't she see what he was *doing*? You didn't talk with a monster like this, didn't bargain with him, because he was never interested in doing more than finding another way to hurt people.

"Then what are you interested in?" Ravin said.

"Do not try my patience," Lenore said. "My friend lies dead at your feet. The only reason I am not having you killed is because that would only keep the violence going. I am not going to be like you."

Erin was sprinting now, bouncing from person to person like a boulder rolling down a hill, ignoring the pain that shot through her with each impact. None of that mattered, only the sight of Ravin there, close enough now to her sister that he could have reached out and touched her. Erin's hand clutched her spear hard enough that her knuckles hurt, and still she kept running.

"No, you are not," Ravin agreed. "Because you will not live that long, Princess."

His blade swept up then, slower than it might have before because of how badly wounded he was, but still with terrifying ease. Too late, Lenore seemed to realize just how close she was to this man who had killed so many of her family, and how far away everyone else was. Odd had died to get her back to safety, yet here she was, stepping willingly into the shadow of Ravin's sword.

Erin ran forward as his blade rose for the killing blow, skidding in between herself and Lenore on her knees, ignoring the agony that the movement brought as she drove herself upward from that kneeling position. Her spear thrust straight up as she powered back to her feet, and it showed just how much Odd had weakened Ravin that he didn't have any time to react.

The point of the spear slammed up into his skull, through its base, up into the brain and out through the back of his head, so that for a moment, he looked like a head set on a spike above a castle's gates, save that his body was still attached to it. Erin held her position, all too aware of the blade hanging over her, with no way to stop it from killing her if it came down in one last strike.

Instead, Ravin stood transfixed, and then the sword clattered from his hands. Erin wasn't done though. She yanked her spear from his skull and brought the long, broad head of it around in a sweep at neck height that took Ravin's head from his shoulders.

"*That's* the only ending to this you deserve," Erin said, staring down at his body.

CHAPTER THIRTY FOUR

D evin lay there as Anders descended the stairs, too battered to move for several moments. In that time, he knew that it would have been easy for Anders to simply jump down and drive the point of Loss through his chest. Instead, he almost sauntered down, into the laboratory area.

"I'm tempted to kick you down the rest of the stairs one by one," Anders said. "It's not that I hate you, or that you're a bad person, but you need to see the difference between us. You need to know why *I'm* the one who has to live, and *you* have to die."

Devin started to rise, but Anders timed a kick that sent him sprawling into the laboratory space, clattering into something as he tried to come up. It turned out to be a metal stand, and Devin managed to get it up between him and Anders in time to deflect the first stroke from Loss, but the sword seemed to cut through the metal as easily as paper, leaving Devin holding the stub of it.

Devin threw it at Anders, but then had to dodge as his foe struck at him again and again. Devin threw himself this way and that, barely dodging each strike, and the worst part was that it was obvious none of the blows was delivered with real intent, each one just forcing him to parry frantically.

Devin tried to strike back at Anders, grabbing a wavy bladed dagger that had been set out for study on one of the tables, but so soon after tumbling down so many stairs he didn't have the strength or the speed for it. Anders parried the blow, pressed in close, and tumbled Devin to the floor over his hip. He looked around for the sword he'd dropped, but couldn't see it. Had it fallen further down the tower?

"I think we've established that I'm a better fighter than you," Anders said.

Devin saw Sigil slinking down the stairs, hobbling slightly.

"Tell the wolf that if it leaps, I'll cut it down," Anders said. "A conduit like that is valuable, but unlike you, I have no need for one. Let me show you."

He made a gesture as Devin started to rise, and now it seemed as if the whole weight of the air was pressing down on his chest, pinning him in place, making it nearly impossible to breathe. Devin fought to grasp the strands of the magic and unravel them, but with the world still spinning from where he'd struck his head on a stair, he couldn't focus enough to do it.

"You don't have my skill in magic, either," Anders said. "Do you know how many hours I trained as a child, being made to repeat incantations over and over, every step designed to bring my mind to the right place to work a spell? My tutors would beat me for failing, and when I complained to my father, *he* beat me for failing to live up to his expectations."

"Am I supposed to ... feel sorry for you?" Devin asked.

"No, you are supposed to understand why some bumbling amateur could never hope to control the forces of this world as perfectly as me," Anders said. "You're supposed to understand that you are *less*."

He paced around Devin. "Do you have any of the knowledge of the House of Scholars? Have you learned anything about dragons like the one that attacked the city?"

Devin shook his head tightly. "I saw one before. I think it was that one."

"You saw one," Anders said with a laugh. He turned as Sigil leapt at him, and the air there threw the wolf back against the wall, pinning him in place. It meant that Devin could stand, just barely managing to dodge another stroke of the sword.

"Do you think you could fit in at court? That you have *any* of the polish or poise needed to persuade people there?" Anders asked.

"I think Princess Lenore thought so," Devin said, but thoughts of her turned his thoughts darker, the hurt of losing her filling up inside him, threatening to spill out in rage.

"What would *you* know about princesses?" Anders demanded, still driving Devin back around the room. "What would you know about *anything*? You're not a rival to me, Devin; you're an insult. You're a boy without training, without skill, without hope. I'll be doing you a favor by killing you, and then I'll set your body here for Master Grey to find, so that it's the last thing he sees before I kill him too."

He lifted the sword, and this time, Devin knew that he wouldn't be swinging Loss at half speed. He stood there, knowing that he was going to die, and there was a part of him that didn't even think it would be so bad, because with Lenore gone, what else was there?

As if something broke inside him, Devin felt his pain and grief pour out, into the sword. He felt them connect with the last bindings he'd put in place as he'd finished it. He'd been so consumed with emptiness and pain when he'd made it that it had been all he'd had left to put into it when he'd finished it off.

Now, his pain met the well of dark energy he'd put into the sword, the emptiness and pain that had gone into the grip and the pommel seeming to answer him in a raw outpouring of power. The pommel glowed with a dark corona of energy that spread out over Anders's hands.

Devin saw Anders wince at that power, and then drop the sword as if just holding it hurt him. It didn't hurt Devin, though, as he snatched it up. Instead, the hurt and the loss inside it fit with him, seemed to fill him with their darkness and their power, so that nothing hurt anymore compared to the deep ache of it.

He lifted the sword, testing it as Anders took a step back from him. There was a look on Anders's face that Devin hadn't expected to see. Horror.

"What ... how can you hold that?" he asked. "How can you bear to?"

Devin could not only bear it; he found that he enjoyed it. There was something pure, something real, about giving in to the despair that had threatened to overwhelm him ever since he had heard about Lenore's death. It sang through him, crying out for vengeance against anyone it could find.

Anders more than deserved it. Poising the sword in front of him, Devin readied himself for the stroke that would end his enemy's life.

Another sword cut down on his, and Devin just had enough time to recognize the other star metal blade he'd made before Loss was knocked from his grip. With it gone, the feelings of despair needing to be filled by violence receded, but only a little.

"We need him, Devin."

Devin looked around to find Master Grey there, holding the sword that Devin had dropped in his tumble down the stairs.

"Why?" Devin demanded. "He attacked me, stole from me. He was going to kill you. Why doesn't he deserve to die?"

"That is the pain talking," Master Grey said. "It was a powerful emotion to put into the sword, but also a dangerous one. You need to fight past it, Devin."

Devin tried, but it seemed to him that all his interactions with Anders to date had been about his supposed rival attacking him for stealing what he saw as his destiny. If he was going to keep coming until he finally succeeded, didn't it make sense to kill him now?

Just that thought was enough to make Devin realize that he wasn't himself. He would never normally have thought about killing someone just because it might save him trouble later on.

"Listen to me, both of you," Master Grey said. "I hid you from one another, but that does not mean that you don't each have your part to play in this. With everything that is to come, you will *both* be needed, if humanity is to survive. If you fall upon one another now, then the whole world will be left without one of those meant to aid it."

"An easy thing to say *now*, sorcerer," Anders snapped.

He moved his hands, and Devin felt him forming the beginnings of a spell. In that moment, it was like he could *see* the way the next few moments would play out, with Anders striking Master Grey out of the way, then snatching up Loss, then...

He felt the moment when Master Grey's magic came down over Anders's like a blanket, smothering the spell before it could start. Devin might have decided against killing him, but that didn't mean he couldn't do anything to hurt him. He stepped forward, swinging his right hand in a straight punch that connected sweetly with Anders's jaw, sending the other young man slumping to the floor in unconsciousness.

"He will be angry when he wakes up," Devin said, rubbing his bruised knuckles.

"I shall contain him until he comes to his senses," Master Grey said. He dragged Anders to the wall and whispered words. Devin felt the lines of power there shift and blend, wrapping around Anders so that the wall seemed almost to absorb him into itself. "He will stay there until we can come to an accord."

Devin suspected that the act of being imprisoned like that would only make Anders angrier, but he was willing to go along with it.

The sorcerer picked up Loss, reversed it, and set it on a table near Devin along with the one he'd made for the wedding. "A blade to be careful with."

Devin couldn't argue with that. Besides, he had more important things to talk to the sorcerer about.

"What did you mean," Devin demanded, "when you said that you needed both of us? Haven't you held back enough now?"

The sorcerer seemed to want to brush that away with a smile, but Devin wasn't in a mood to let it go. He was about to ask again, when the sound of raised voices filtered in from outside the castle. They were chanting one thing, over and over again.

"Queen Lenore. Queen Lenore..."

Devin's eyes widened at that chant, barely able to take in the possibility of what it might mean.

"No," he breathed. "It *can't* be."

CHAPTER THIRTY FIVE

"Q ueen Lenore! Queen Lenore!"

Lenore felt almost like she was floating above herself as she started to lead everyone back to the city. There were so many emotions roiling inside her that in some ways it was simpler to just focus on walking, snatching up her banner from where she'd planted it, carrying it into the city.

Greave and Erin moved into place beside her, while half a dozen others carried Odd's body on a stretcher made from spears and cloaks, carrying him with them so that even in death he could play his part in this. Lenore saw Aurelle walking a little way away from Greave. She didn't know what had happened between them, and she couldn't stop the progress of the army to find out. She just had to trust that things would be all right.

It wasn't exactly an army now, because it consisted of soldiers from both sides, along with all the common folk who had come out to help them. An army would have fallen upon the city, tearing into it and taking what it wanted. Lenore would have done anything to stop that.

This was more like a procession. People lined the streets, and Lenore heard her name chanted over and over.

"Queen Lenore! Queen Lenore!"

A child threw flowers her way, and Lenore caught them, laughing in sudden joy. They seemed like a far better thing to hold than a sword. The joy cut through some of the other things she was feeling: grief for those who had fallen, anger that Ravin hadn't taken her final offer of peace, fear at all the things that might still need to be done.

The gates to the city hung open, and they made their way through. People peered down at them from windows, some looking on with fear because they didn't know what was going on, more waving and smiling because they did. Still, Lenore advanced to the sound of her own name echoing from every side.

They processed up toward the castle, and this was the part that Lenore dreaded. She'd seen for herself how prepared the castle could be for an attack, how easily the keep in particular might be defended. If some of Ravin's people decided that they wanted to hold out, then this could turn into a bloody siege within her own city.

Yet, when they reached the castle, they found the gates as open as those of the city. Figures stood there, waiting for them, and Lenore saw Master Grey there standing next to ... to Devin.

Lenore rushed forward and just stared at him.

"Devin, you're ..."

"You're alive," he breathed, looking as shocked as she felt.

There were so many things she wanted to say in that moment, so many feelings that she wanted to express that it felt as if she couldn't find the words to contain them.

"I ..." she began.

"Lenore," Devin said, "I thought ... I thought you were ..."

Lenore suspected that they could have stood there forever, neither quite managing to say anything, so she did the only thing she could think of. She threw her arms around him, kissing him before she could think about it long enough to stop herself. She knew that a queen shouldn't kiss someone born so far beneath her, yet ... yet she wanted to. She wanted to do so much more than that. She was almost surprised when Devin kissed her back.

She could have stayed like that forever, except that Lenore could see Erin there, advancing angrily on someone with her spear in her hand.

"Later," Lenore said, as she broke away from Devin. "I ... later."

She would have said more, but she saw Vars there, his hands up as if that would stop Erin from doing anything. A woman in common clothes stood between them now, dagger drawn, and she seemed to be the only reason that Erin wasn't able to cut their brother down.

Given all he'd done, Lenore was tempted to let her. Even so, she made herself step forward, taking hold of the haft of the spear and looking her sister in the eye.

"Hasn't there been enough killing for one day?" she asked, with a pointed look back toward the stretcher where Odd lay. It was enough to make Erin lower her spear.

"Fine," Erin said. "For now."

Lenore turned to the woman, who was still standing there, dagger drawn. "What's your name?"

"Bethe, your majesty," the woman said.

"And you helped to take the castle?"

The woman nodded.

"Then you have my thanks, Bethe," Lenore said.

"It was Vars's idea," she blurted.

Lenore looked over to her brother, trying to guess at his reasoning, then decided that this wasn't the moment.

"Still, it was brave to come here." She turned her attention to Master Grey. "And you, sorcerer, what role did you play in all this?"

"Your majesty," Master Grey said, with a nod that was probably as close as the sorcerer ever got to respect. "The smallest of parts. Still, there are things that I will need to speak to you about."

"Soon," Lenore promised. There were things that she needed to do first.

She led the way to the keep, and to the great hall within. The people there thronged it. Lenore made out Lady Meredith moving her way toward the front. She had no doubt that there were things that the mistress of the House of Sighs would want. Others would too, and almost automatically her eyes fell on the bulky form of Lord Welles, the younger frame of Lord Ness.

"Wait here," she commanded, and started to head out of the hall.

"Lenore," Erin said, starting to follow, but Lenore cut her off with a shake of the head.

"Stay here," she said to her sister. "Please."

"What if there are Quiet Men?" Erin asked.

Lenore shrugged. "Their emperor is dead. Any left will probably be running by now, or they'll want to blend in and disappear. Stay here, organize things for Odd. Greave will do most of the rest, but you do that. See that his body is treated with honor."

That was enough to make her sister nod, and Lenore headed for the doors that led up into the depths of the keep. She briefly glanced back toward Devin, wishing that she could invite him to come with her, but the reasons she wanted him there had nothing to do with this moment.

She went up to her old rooms, opening the doors and just standing there. It didn't matter right then that the furniture wasn't where she'd left it, or that the richer hangings had been stripped away since she'd left. What mattered was the smell of it and the feel of the place around her.

She went to the balcony, which looked out over the city. From there, Lenore could hear that the chanting of her name still continued in the city, along with what sounded like music and the beginning of celebrations. At the same time, she could see the destruction that had been wrought in Royalsport, and the battlefield that lay beyond its boundaries.

Lenore shuddered at the sight of it all, and that was part of the reason she'd wanted to do this part alone. She hadn't wanted anyone to see the tears on her face as she looked out on the piles of corpses that littered the battlefield. So many deaths seemed like a high price to pay, even to get her home back.

The interior of the city looked almost as bad. Lenore didn't know the cause, but it looked as if large parts of Royalsport had been on fire in the recent past. Buildings lay blackened and fallen into rubble, while the gates on the east and west of the city were broken.

The enormity of everything that she would have to do next hit Lenore then. Yes, she'd just beaten Ravin, but that didn't mean that things just stopped. Large sections of the city were in ruins, needing to be rebuilt. The bodies from the battlefield would need to be buried, and the families of the dead cared for. Lenore would have to send out messengers to announce what had happened, and maybe send out forces to deal with any pockets of Ravin's soldiers who still clung onto positions they'd taken within her kingdom.

There would need to be discussions about the nobles who had supported Ravin but then turned away from him. There would need to be arrangements to get those of Ravin's soldiers who had given up back to the Southern Kingdom. The long bridges across the Slate would need to be rebuilt. As the queen, Lenore would need to be the one who arranged those things. She would have help, of course, but ultimately the responsibility would fall to her.

Could she do it? Winning a throne was almost the easy part compared to ruling a kingdom. Even so, Lenore was willing to give it everything she had. She felt, in a lot of ways, like she'd prepared for this moment all her life.

When Lenore went down to the great hall again, people were already starting to organize some of it. Greave was giving instructions to those of the servants who remained, while Erin seemed to be giving orders to the guards, making sure that the city was secure. Lord Welles and Lord Ness were surrounded by their own people, while many of the common folk were standing staring, as if wondering what they should do next.

A cheer went up as Lenore stepped into the room.

"The queen!" a voice called, and Lenore didn't have to look hard to spot Lady Meredith shouting it.

"The queen!" the others there roared back.

Lenore stepped over to the throne that had been her father's, before it had been taken by her brother, her mother, and Ravin. She stood in front of it, looking out over the crowd, seeing the friends there, but also the people she would need to talk to and placate, command, and in some cases punish for all they had done.

"My friends," she said, "we have come a long way. We have fought an enemy who overwhelmed our kingdom, and we won. We won for many reasons. I was lucky enough to be able to find allies. I've had friends and followers who have been brave and skilled. One of the finest warriors the kingdom has seen died to bring it about, and my brother crafted a strategy that fooled even a master general like King Ravin."

She paused, looking out over all of them there. "In truth, though, we would not have won without all of you. You are the ones who came to the kingdom's aid when it needed you most. You are the ones who ended the battle, and took back this kingdom. I will rule for all of you, and I will not forget what you did."

As the people cheered, Lenore lowered herself onto the throne.

Tomorrow, there would be so much to do.

But for now, she was the only ruler left in the Northern Kingdom.

It was, finally, done.

She was queen.

Epilogue

Nerra rode on the back of Shadr the dragon queen, reveling in the power of her flight and the anticipation of what was to come. Below her, a human settlement stood, soldiers sitting there as they guarded a precious stack of resources.

Nerra couldn't even remember what they were, or why they'd selected this place from all the others they could have struck. Caught up in the anticipation coming from Shadr, Nerra could barely think about anything except the violence to come.

The great black dragon swooped down, flames pouring from her mouth to wash over everything beneath her. The dragon's roar sent human things scurrying like ants, and Nerra's roar matched Shadr's own, primal and filling the sky around her.

Some part of her told her that this was wrong, that the sight of humans burning like candles should fill her with disgust, even loathing, yet Nerra couldn't even begin to remember why. With Shadr's battle frenzy running through her, she reveled in the destruction.

It wasn't just Shadr's rage. Deep inside, Nerra had found her own to match it.

Nerra roared out her anger at her father sending her away, abandoning her to try to protect himself and the others after a life where he'd kept so much about her hidden away. He'd been ashamed of her all her life, and Nerra's anger couldn't forgive that.

She roared her anger at her family: Vars for his cowardice, Rodry for treating the world like it was something to hunt or fight with, Lenore for being so perfect all the time. She screamed out at Greave always being in a library rather than being there for her, and Erin for always wanting to fight.

She cried out her rage at her mother for not helping her, at her family for not standing by her, at her entire kingdom for treating her like something that was ... less.

She was not less.

She was more, so much more.

She watched the fires burn below in a line of flame that seemed to cut across the kingdom, and it didn't even begin to feel like enough.

Soon, *soon*, she would ride that wave of fire all the way to Royalsport.

And the throne that lay waiting there for her.

NOW AVAILABLE FOR PRE-ORDER!

SHIELD OF DRAGONS
(Age of the Sorcerers—Book Seven)

"Has all the ingredients for an instant success: plots, counterplots, mystery, valiant knights, and blossoming relationships replete with broken hearts, deception and betrayal. It will keep you entertained for hours, and will satisfy all ages. Recommended for the permanent library of all fantasy readers."
—Books and Movie Reviews, Roberto Mattos (re The Sorcerer's Ring)

"The beginnings of something remarkable are there."
—San Francisco Book Review (re A Quest of Heroes)

From #1 bestseller Morgan Rice, author of A Quest of Heroes (over 1,300 five star reviews) comes a startlingly new fantasy series. SHIELD OF DRAGONS is book #7 in bestselling author Morgan Rice's new epic fantasy series, Age of the Sorcerers, which begins with book #1 (THRONE OF DRAGONS), a #1 bestseller with dozens of five-star reviews—and a free download!

In SHIELD OF DRAGONS (Age of the Sorcerers—Book Seven), Lenore must try to restore a fractured kingdom. Hidden enemies surround her, all vying for power, while a mysterious new adversary rises in the South, requiring Erin to be dispatched on a fateful mission to stop it. All the while, Nerra and her dragons thirst for vengeance, while Lenore longs to be reunited with Devin—but a tragic twist may shatter all of their plans.

AGE OF THE SORCERERS weaves an epic sage of love, of passion, of sibling rivalry; of rogues and hidden treasure; of monks and warriors; of honor and glory, and of betrayal, fate and destiny. It is a tale you will not put down until the early hours, one that will transport you to another world and have you fall in in love with characters you will never forget. It appeals to all ages and genders.

Book #8 will be available soon.

"A spirited fantasy ….Only the beginning of what promises to be an epic young adult series."
                                        —Midwest Book Review (re A Quest of Heroes)

"Action-packed …. Rice's writing is solid and the premise intriguing."
                                        —Publishers Weekly (re A Quest of Heroes)

SHIELD OF DRAGONS
(Age of the Sorcerers—Book Seven)

Did you know that I've written multiple series? If you haven't read all my series, click the image below to download a series starter!